HODDER CHILDREN'S BOOKS

First published in Great Britain in 2020 by Hodder and Stoughton

5 7 9 10 8 6 4

Text and illustrations copyright © Nick East, 2020

The moral rights of the author and illustrator have been asserted.

A CIP catalogue record for this book is available from the British Library.

ISBN 978 1 444 94530 0

Printed and bound in Great Britain by Clays Ltd, Elcograph S.p.A.
The paper and board used in this book are made from wood from
responsible sources

Hodder Children's Books
An imprint of Hachette Children's Group
Part of Hodder and Stoughton
Carmelite House
50 Victoria Embankment
London EC4Y 0DZ
An Hachette UK Company
www.hachette.co.uk
www.hachettechildrens.co.uk

-NICK EAST-

AGENT WEASEL

AND THE ABOMINABLE DR SNOW

I ♥ WI6

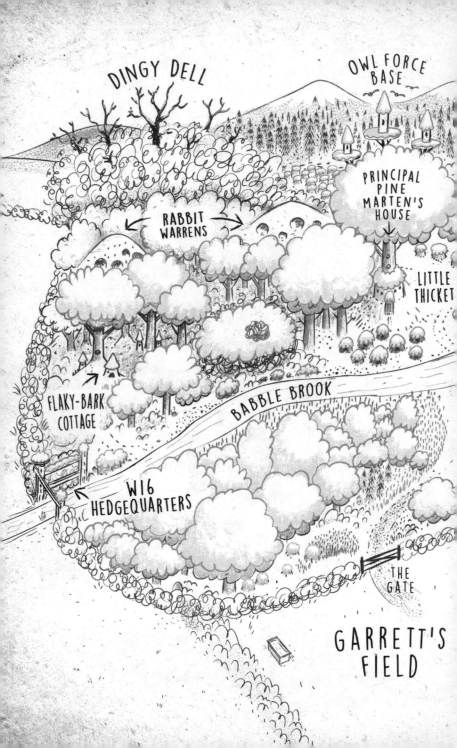

FOR TIM.
KEEP THAT AGENT WEASEL SPIRIT GOING
AND BATTLE ON THROUGH.
YOUR LOVING BRO Nx

In a forgotten corner of the countryside
lies a small green wood, much like any other.
But take a closer look and it is far from ordinary.
For this is the United Woodlands – home of
Agent Weasel, legendary super-spy. A place full
of adventure, mystery – and an incredibly
wide variety of edible nuts.

CHAPTER 1

Weasel awoke in a complete and utter stew. Not the type you have with fluffy dumplings, carrots and a thick scrummy gravy. The kind of stew where your head spins, your eyes bulge and things do not feel quite as they should.

He sat bolt upright, wringing his fuzzy morning brain for an answer. Did he have somewhere to be or something important to do?

Throwing back the covers, Weasel leapt from the bed and crashed over a big solid object in the way … *CLUNK–BANG–CLOSH!*

'PRICKLY BUM THISTLES, who put that there?' cried Weasel. In the dim light he could just make out a bulky travel trunk next to his bed. A variety of woolly items poked out from beneath the lid.

Ahhhhh! That will be me, then, he recalled.

Weasel had been frantically packing the previous evening, though he couldn't remember what for. And after a particularly busy day of spying, he must have collapsed on the bed and fallen into a deep sleep.

Being a woodland super-spy could be awfully tiring. And poor Agent Weasel had just about spied himself to exhaustion yesterday. But why the trunk? And what was the niggle at the back of his foggy mind?

Lying snout down on the rickety floorboards, Weasel squinted out through the frosty upstairs window of his top-secret home, Flaky-Bark Cottage. Thick snow covered every inch of the United Woodlands in a sparkly silence.

He smiled to himself with a happy little glow in his chest. Weasel loved snow. And while most animals were tucked up in toasty dens – hibernating through the chilly winter – for Weasel it was a wondrous time to be up and about … Then it hit him.

'SNOW – OH GOSH!'

He had somewhere to be and something

VERY important to do!

Scrambling back over the trunk, Weasel grabbed the alarm clock from the bedside table. Ten past seven. *YICKERTY—YIKES*, he thought, *twenty minutes before the team arrive*. There was just enough time to get his kit together and have a bite of breakfast. Weasel could barely contain his excitement – for this was a very special morning indeed!

Every two winters, just after Christmas, groups of plucky animals gathered on the legendary Windtop Hill. They travelled from far and wide for one thing and one thing only – to compete in the best international alpine sports event around, the mighty WINTER WHOPPER GAMES!

This year Woodland Intelligence – or WI6 to you and me – had entered its own crack squad of elite athletes. And Agent Weasel, being one of its most renowned super-spies, had been given the honour of captaining Team United Woodlands.

Little did he know that the selection committee (which consisted of only Principal Pine Marten, leader of the United Woodlands, and H, head-honcho hedgehog at WI6) struggled to find any other animal to do it!

With some reluctance, the pair eventually decided on Weasel. Their hesitation had nothing to do with his ability to get the job done. Agent Weasel had a glowing record. The problem was his absolute refusal to do things by the book. And doing things by the book at WI6 was of the utmost importance. Even if that book did weigh a ton and was impossible to drag around on tricky spy operations.

Weasel had no knowledge of any of this. And as much as he loved his job, protecting his woodland home from all sorts of crooked and mysterious mischief, this was a privilege beyond anything else. He felt like the luckiest weasel ever!

GOSH, look at the time! He seriously needed to get his skates on! As the captain, it was essential he was ready and waiting when the squad pulled up at his front gate.

He whipped open the trunk lid to check his winter essentials. Without warning, a fluttering dart shot out and hovered right between his eyes.

'MURIEL!' exclaimed Weasel. 'What on earth were you doing in there?'

Muriel was Agent Weasel's personally trained, elite homing moth. A rather excellent and trusty companion, she had got him out of some tricky old scrapes on a number of occasions. Muriel perched on the end of Weasel's nose, with an especially bad-tempered scowl on her mothy little brow.

'Hmmmm!' said Weasel, plucking one of his best fluffy socks from the trunk and holding it up to the wintery light. It was now more holes than sock. Muriel did a small apologetic shrug, as if to say, 'If you accidentally shut me in a travel trunk overnight, I'm going to have to eat!'

WHIRRRR

Ah well, no harm done, he thought. *Good old Grannie Weasel will soon knit me another pair of these bad boys.* Weasel did a quick last inspection:

Woolly items in order ... CHECK!

Muriel safe and clear of woolly items ... CHECK!

Hot chocolate and marshmallows for team morale ... CHECK!

SLAM—CLUNK!

Trunk locked and secure ... CHECK!

Muriel furiously flapped her wings, in an attempt to catch Weasel's attention.

Er ... was there something missing?

She was perched on an open notebook lying on the bedside table and fluttered to his shoulder as he picked it up.

Weasel kept it there to scribble down night-time thoughts. Although remembering to read it in the morning was the tricky bit. In tired, wobbly letters, it said:

NETTLE TEA
PINE SLUDGE HAIR GEL
BISCUITS
(THE NICE ONES WITH STRIPY ICING ON TOP)

He hadn't finished reading the short shopping list when he noticed the big black letters scrawled below. He must have written them in the middle of the night. An icy chill filled his tummy as he read:

VERY, VERY IMPORTANT!
DO NOT FORGET TO COLLECT
BARKBOARD SUPER—SLIDER
FROM HEDGEQUARTERS!

'OH NO!' despaired Weasel.

The barkboard was his main event at the games. He had entered for the downhill race and the freestyle jump competitions. And without his beloved board he wouldn't be doing much of either! The clock was ticking. There was nothing for it. He would need to make a quick dash over to Hedgequarters, grab the board and get back before Team United Woodlands arrived.

'Let's go, Muriel – no time to waste!' And in a blink of a gnat's eye, the pair raced off to brave the outdoor winter chill.

CHAPTER 2

Weasel scampered between heavily snow-caked trees towards Hedgequarters, the WI6 command post – named after the actual hedge in which it was based. But Weasel found focusing on the task in paw difficult. The image of a triple fir-cone medal sparkling around his neck repeatedly popped up in his mind. It was the ultimate prize at the Winter Whopper Games and Weasel had never quite managed to win it.

Each cone on the medal stood for a particular quality required from the heroic athlete. One being bravery – of course. Two was loyalty – which goes without saying. And three was the absolute necessity to be completely off your rocker.

Weasel had all three in bucket loads. And without any spy stuff to distract him this year, he had to be in with a chance.

Suddenly Weasel realised how quiet it had become as he trotted along. There was not a sound – literally not a dickie bird. Muricl's whirring wings and the crunchy *squeak, squeak* of Weasel's snowshoes were the only things to be heard.

To call the things on Weasel's paws snowshoes was stretching the truth a little. They were actually an old pair of shuttlebop rackets. It was a popular game in the United Woodlands, generally played in summer, which involved whacking an acorn backwards and forwards over Babble Brook until the acorn got lodged in a tree or a competitor went head-over-heels into the stream. The rackets doubled as pretty top-notch snow gear.

They dodged their way through an eerie-looking bramble thicket and Weasel's spy senses began to tingle. Were they being watched? *It must be my imagination playing tricks*, he was

SQUEAK
SQUEAK

thinking ... when a sudden and very large
shadow passed over the glittering white snow.

EEK! Weasel snapped his head skywards, but saw nothing. Maybe it was a passing cloud, or one of those scatter-brained squirrels searching for nuts. Then out of the blue ... *WHUMPF!*

Everything went dark.

Weasel took a few moments to get his bearings. Was he under the snow? Well, it certainly felt chilly enough. Now he knew how a Popsicle felt in a freezer!

He pushed in what he thought was an upright direction and popped his head out into fresh woodland air ...

POOOF!

Taking a deep breath, he scanned the woods through narrowed eyes. There was nobody there, not even Muriel. She must have flown on to Hedgequarters – not realising he was up to his neck in it.

As he struggled to get free, it soon became clear the shuttlebop rackets would not budge. *SHIVERING SQUIRREL TAILS*, he thought. *If I don't wriggle out of here soon, I'll become a weasel-shaped Popsicle!*

Then he heard *crump, crump, crump, crump* – trudging footsteps from behind!

Weasel froze, which wasn't too difficult in his current predicament. The footsteps came to a halt just behind the back of his head. If only he could get a paw free. But it was no good – he was well and truly packed in.

Was this an ambush? If so, he would need

some serious Weasel charm to wriggle his way out of this one.

As he mulled over something witty and spy-like to say, he felt a strange warming sensation all over his body. The weight of the snow seemed to lighten. Weasel gave a quick jiggle, and the shuttlebop rackets were free. He vaulted into the air with a determined flip, landing paws up in the snow … *SHUMMMF!*

'YEOW!' he shrieked in surprise.

The strangest stubby creature stood before him. The unfortunate thing looked like an explosion at a grannies' knitting convention. It wore an oversized woolly hat with a giant pom-pom perched on top. The scarf wrapped around its body was the size of a boa constrictor. But most unusual of all were the humongous mittens sticking out at either

side. One blast of the cold north wind and the creature would be sailing off over the treetops!

The whatsit waddled forward with outstretched arms. Weasel leapt back, his paws up ready for action.

'The name's Weasel, Agent Weasel!' he snarled, hoping to scare the critter off.

But it just shrugged, sniffed and mumbled, 'Beasel it'ffs be, Moorkins.'

What kind of language was this, puzzled Weasel? He'd once met a Peruvian guinea pig with a similar accent. But there was something slightly familiar about …

Suddenly the thingamabob reached under its hat. Weasel tensed, expecting an attack. But his foe pulled out a large, crusty, green hanky, and blew very loudly indeed.

PAAAAAAAAAAARP!

'Who in DAINTY BLUEBELL WOOD are you?' demanded Weasel.

The woolly mound pulled off a giant mitten and a tiny paw dragged down the now rather snotty scarf, revealing a long, red, sniffling nose.

'Like I said, Weasel, it's me, Doorkins – sniff!'

'HA HA, my old chum! I would never have guessed!' cried Weasel with glee.

Doorkins the dormouse was Weasel's best pal in the whole world. He had lived in the tree above Flaky-Bark Cottage since they were both tiny fluff-balls.

Weasel squeezed his little buddy in a badger-like hug, causing a *YA—AAACHOOO!* The mighty sneeze was loud enough to wake a bear! Not that the United Woodlands had any bears. But if it did, the sneeze would most certainly have woken them!

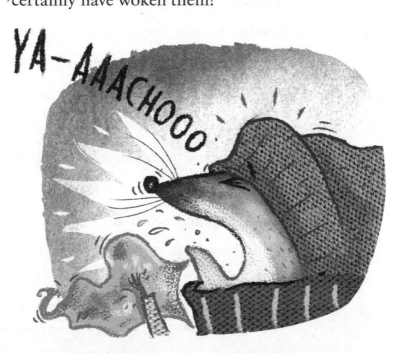

'What in COBBLER'S name are you doing out here?' Weasel asked, rubbing the sneezy wet patch off his jumper.

'Ah! Sorry about that, old chap.' Doorkins nodded guiltily. 'Bit of a sniffle, don't you know. I was following you!'

Doorkins had been outside cracking hazelnuts for his friends the blue tits who were flying in for breakfast that morning when he saw Weasel suddenly storm off through the cottage gate. He knew Team United Woodlands were due at any moment and Weasel dashing off like that could only mean trouble!

'What's with the big mittens?' asked Weasel.

'Ah, well!' said Doorkins, waggling one of the flipper-like gloves around. 'These are WI6 Mega Mittens! Designed to keep paws warm – and melt snow and ice at a touch. I'm giving them a trial run for the Boffin Bunnies – SNIFF.'

'Ah-ha, so that's how you thawed me out of the snow pile!' Those Boffin Bunnies at WI6 Hedgequarters were clever little fluffies, thought Weasel. They came up with all sorts of brilliant gadgets for needy agents. It was hard to imagine spy-life without them.

With a whirr and a flutter, Muriel plonked down on Weasel's shoulder. She gave him a withering look, as if to say, 'Where in the Dingy Dell have you been?' Then she clocked Doorkins in his woollen outfit.

Her eyes widened and she smacked her lips in a hungry kind of way. The poor dormouse backed off nervously.

'Ah yes, sorry about that, old chum,'

apologised Weasel. 'Muriel's developed a taste for the woolly stuff recently. Anyway, I'd love to stay and chat, but I need to grab my barkboard from Hedgequarters and—'

Doorkins held up a floppy mitten. 'But, Weasel,' he said with a puzzled look, 'I picked up your board yesterday. I went to put it in the cottage cupboard but—'

'WHAAAAAAT!' cried Weasel, cutting Doorkins off. He shot back towards home as fast as his shuttlebop rackets could carry him. Doorkins gave a big sigh and waddled along after the frantic super-spy.

CHAPTER 3

Weasel charged in through the front door.

BOOOM—CRASH!

Panting heavily, he looked at the clock on the mantelpiece – he had two minutes until the team arrived. Poor Weasel felt a cold sweat coming on.

Without a thought for the rackets strapped to his paws, he clattered across the room to the cupboard door. He was about to grab the handle ... then thought twice and paused.

This particular cupboard wasn't just any old cupboard, it was the infamous cupboard of DOOM, since Weasel felt complete and utter doom every time he went near it. It was so crammed full of stuff, it was a major incident waiting to happen!

Weasel took a deep breath. 'Take it steady, old chap,' he whispered to himself. With a shaky paw, he reached for the doorknob … just as Doorkins and Muriel burst in.

CREAK

'NO, WEASEL, NOT IN THERE!' cried Doorkins in a high-pitched squeak.

But as Weasel whipped round in surprise, his elbow brushed the cupboard handle.

RUMBLE, RUMBLE, RUMBLE!

BOOOOM!

The cupboard door flew open and a great wave of bric-à-brac rolled out ... taking Weasel and his shuttlebop rackets with it.

Doorkins and Muriel leapt for the staircase as the tsunami of clutter thundered past. It rumbled out of the front door and came to a halt in the deep snow. Agent Weasel lay there dazed, staring up at the fluffy white clouds floating by.

'Hello, old chap. Doing a spot of avalanche training I see,' said a jolly voice from the direction of the cottage gate.

'MOLE!' Weasel cried with joy.

Agent Mole waddled up the path with an amused smirk on her face. 'Let me help you out of there, my dear fellow,' she said, offering him a large shovel-like paw.

As WI6 agents go, Mole was one of the best. And she was without doubt the most trustworthy of all-round goody-good eggs that there possibly could be.

'We're ready for the off, Captain!' she said with a beam. Mole thumbed over to the front gate, where, to Weasel's delight, the magnificent Team United Woodlands snow pedal sled stood. So called as it required frantic pedalling to make it go!

And go it did. Two powerful rear-mounted propellers, made from dried sycamore seeds, twirled to drive it forward. It was absolutely essential that you held on to scarfs, hats and tails – anything that dangled too close could get a bit shredded!

A mostly familiar bunch of creatures sat in the sled.

Corporal Steadfast of the Stag Beetle Special Ops Regiment stood to attention and snapped a quick salute, with three very smart and shiny black insect troopers following her example. Weasel saluted back, giving a friendly wink to his good friend and comrade Steadfast.

Next to them, with a big toothy grin, was former Fiendish Fox Gang member Viv – now WI6 friend and first time snowball dodge competitor. Vic, Viv's bad-tempered whiny twin, had not been selected for the team. He'd apparently gone off in a huff – maybe in hunt of something sweet and cake-like to eat. Which was probably for the best.

Then there was a sleek white stranger, perched elegantly at the back of the sled.

'That's a white ermine from the northern forest,' whispered Doorkins. 'A distant cousin of Principal Pine Marten – I'm not sure of her name. She's filling in for Chef Flourplop, who unfortunately chafed his bottom in a nasty grating accident!'

'Er … what's an ermine?' muttered Weasel dozily.

'It's really a type of stoat,' Doorkins explained, 'pretty much identical to a weasel apart from the black end to its tail. It's a tiny bit bigger. And its coat goes completely white in winter. Oh, and they are very cool, clever and fearless. So err … similarish – sort of.'

Weasel stared at the ermine with admiration. She wore a splendid red polo-neck jumper. *What thoroughly good taste*, he thought. She had a tam-o-shanter beret on her head and a pair of round spectacle sunglasses perched on her nose. She looked over them disapprovingly at the mess around the cottage door.

He was just considering introducing himself when …

'Weasel … Weasel … Weeeeasel!' Doorkins whispered forcefully.

'Wha-wha … pardon?' Weasel stuttered distractedly.

'Your barkboard!' Doorkins handed him a long oval sheet of ridged bark. It had a beautifully polished wooden underside and the skilfully carved initials 'AW' in the middle.

'My Super Slider!' exclaimed Weasel. 'It was in the cupboard after all then?'

'Erm … not quite,' admitted Doorkins in a quiet voice. 'It was under your bed – I really daren't touch that rickety old cupboard,

Weasel. I did try to tell you!'

'BOGGLING BARKBUSTERS … after all that mucking about as well!' he said in despair. Weasel felt a tap on his shoulder.

'Sorry, old chap, but we need to get a wriggle on,' urged Mole. 'We've got to reach Beaver Lodge by tonight.'

OOOOH, Beaver Lodge! thought Weasel, perking up.

The journey to Windtop Hill was going to be a long one, so an overnight stop with the jolly old Beavers was just the ticket. He had stayed at Beaver Lodge on a number of trips north and their hospitality was legendary. The thought of their speciality – scrummy mushroom and truffle pie – made his tummy rumble. Particularly as his all-important breakfast had been missed.

They hauled Weasel's trunk on to the WI6 pedal sled and shoved all the cupboard clutter under the rug, leaving a small carpet-covered mountain in the middle of the sitting room.

Weasel and Mole jumped on the sled at the front, since they were the speediest pedallers. Doorkins and Muriel took the seat next to the ermine. The stand-offish creature frowned at the greedy moth as she nibbled away at poor Doorkins's pom-pom.

And with an excited high five from all –
except the nameless ermine, who appeared to
be way too cool for that kind of thing – they
were off, swooshing away from Flaky-Bark
Cottage to the mighty WINTER WHOPPER
GAMES!

CHAPTER 4

Team United Woodlands clung on to the WI6 pedal sled as tightly as they could. It swished along at a fair old pace with Weasel and Mole spinning ten to the dozen.

A strong breeze seemed to pick up from nowhere, coating the unfortunate passengers in clouds of billowing snow like a batch of freshly iced buns.

'I'm f-f-freezing,' shook Viv, her pointy teeth chattering uncontrollably.

Doorkins and Muriel huddled together behind the large fox, the little moth still chewing holes in the dormouse's knitwear for comfort.

Steadfast and her trusty squad bravely tried to remain upright against the cutting wind. But the plucky beetles eventually gave up being macho soldiers, and desperately clung together for warmth.

The only passenger somehow unaffected was the mysterious ermine. The barrage of sharp icy particles appeared to avoid her completely. She sat back, as relaxed as could be, hardly twitching an eyebrow against the terrible chill.

Agent Weasel glanced over his shoulder with a big beaming smile. There was nothing better than an exhilarating jaunt through snowy woodland. But his grin soon faded as he clocked the animal-shaped Popsicles to the rear. He wrenched on the birch-bark air brakes, bringing the sled skidding to a halt.

'FROZEN FURBALLS! My dear fellows, I had no idea!' Weasel cried, leaping down only to plop up to his eyes in deep snow. *Hmmm, hardly halfway to Beaver Lodge and this lot need defrosting already*, he thought, beginning to doubt the hardiness of his teammates.

'The chocolate, Weasel?' Agent Mole suggested as she dragged him out of the snowy pothole.

Weasel frowned. 'Thanks, Mole, but er ... I

don't think we have a chocolate weasel …'

'No, the hot chocolate!' Mole whispered with raised eyebrows.

'Ah yes, of course.' Weasel stuck a paw up his WI6 spy pullover

and pulled out a … small fire extinguisher!

It was fair to say that Weasel had a lot of useful things up his jumper, but in regards to heating up hot chocolate, the extinguisher was not one of them. He fished around again, concentrating hard … and out came a hairdryer. Close but not quite.

His poor teammates were shaking like

maracas at a salsa party. Something had to be done!

'Er, d-don't w-worry, everyone,' sniffed a shivery Doorkins, still suffering with his winter lurgy. 'In my s-satchel there are t-two large flasks of the c-chocolatiest hot chocolate ever – help yourselves!'

'My good friend, you are a lifesaver!' exclaimed Weasel fondly, patting his poor sniffling chum on the back.

'YAAACHOOOO!' sneezed the diddy dormouse.

Doorkins's HC was legendary. Weasel cracked open the marshmallows and passed round steaming mugs of chocolatey goodness. It was gratefully supped by everyone except the ermine.

'No, not for me,' she uttered in a suitably frosty way.

Well, at least she speaks, thought Weasel. *Maybe this ermine is allergic to hot chocolate. How awful would that be?* He shuddered at the possibility.

He decided to pluck up the courage to ask her name – but Viv piped up before he could.

'Are there any chocolate sprinkles? I always have sprinkles with me hot chocolate.'

Viv's twin brother Vic usually did all the complaining. But in his absence, it seemed Viv had taken on the role of moaning Minnie. First whinging about the cold, now this – it was most unlike her.

Much to her delight, Weasel produced a tin of Dr Pops's Most Excellent Chocolate Sprinkles from his hefty travel trunk – plus a variety of woolly items to keep his teammates toasty for the rest of the journey.

Then they were off again, heading directly into the low winter sunshine. The breeze died as the sled climbed up on to Bentbark Ridge – the speediest route to Beaver Lodge by far, or so Weasel claimed. Other team members begged to differ. It was generally known as the risky option.

The group, now revived, were in good spirits, and Steadfast and the beetles kicked off a sing-along. Everyone began to bellow heartily, except the white ermine – singing was obviously not her thing. Weasel wondered if she just felt a bit left out, as he joined in the rousing chorus, hoping she might partake.

Now singing wasn't, and would never be, Weasel's strong point. He was a member of the WI6 Agent choir, who were known for their particularly loud and out-of-tune vocals. As he pedalled furiously, Weasel wailed away like a good 'un! The other animals pretended not to notice, stuffing their ears with anything woolly to hand. The ermine stared in shock and wonderment at the unearthly racket.

Then Weasel stopped abruptly, to everyone's surprise and relief. 'Did anyone see that?' he said with a frown.

'See what?' replied Mole, who was concentrating on steering a straight line along the precarious ridge.

A large shadow had passed across the snowy track just ahead. Weasel thought back to this morning's big scary shadow incident and got a bad feeling about this. Snapping his eyes up to the darkening sky, he saw ... absolutely nothing!

'CLATTERING CANKER-ROOTS,' he said, 'there's something fishy going on here.'

CHOR, CHOR, CHOR! came a panicked crowing sound so loud that everybody practically jumped out of their fur. The source soon became clear, as a squawking green-gold bird tumbled out on to the path up ahead. Weasel recognised him immediately, from the single mangy pheasant feather for a tail (due

to a close call with a particularly rowdy fox) and the fact he delivered post to Flaky-Bark Cottage every morning.

It was Postie Phil.

'PHIIIIIIIL, SHIFT!' screeched Weasel.

Phil looked up with a startled jolt. He tried to scramble to his feet, but it was too late. Mole slammed the steering lever to the right, just missing the horrified bird by a feather. The sled flew off the narrow ridge, speeding down through deep snow!

'DON'T PANIC, EVERYONE!' Weasel cried. 'WE HAVE THIS UNDER CONTROL!'

He pulled hard on the birch-bark air brakes, but the lever snapped off with a loud *CRAAACK!* Everybody locked eyes for an instant, then …

'AAAAAAAARGH!' All panic let loose.

Steadfast and her beetle crew immediately took to the air.

'YIPPEE!' they cried, enjoying the unexpected excitement as they held on to the sled rails, their wings buzzing powerfully in reverse. But the big cumbersome thing would just not slow down … and plunged through a large snow pile, flinging the poor beetles off.

'WEEEEEEEEE!' they yelled, plopping down into the snow one by one. Stag beetles were a bit weird like that.

As the sled burst out the other side, the remaining teammates looked back to see a perfect Team-United-Woodlands-shaped hole in the snow.

Viv grinned. 'PHEW-WEE – that could have been wor— OOOOOOOOF!'

The big fox slammed into a low branch as the sled swooshed away in a cloud of fine glittery ice.

Weasel and Mole, seeing their teammates disappearing one by one, battled to control the careering W16 vehicle as it headed straight for Sheerdrop Cliff. The pair needed to do something, and fast!

From the back of the sled, the composed ermine performed the most sudden and incredible paw flip, vaulting right over Doorkins to the driving position at the front.

THWUMP! Plonking down between the struggling WI6 agents, she grabbed the steering lever, slamming it over to the left. The sled lurched towards a large cheese-shaped wedge of rock between two trees.

WHOOSH! They flew up the rock, launched into the air and everything fell eerily silent. Doorkins gave Muriel – now hovering nearby – a strange little wave as they sailed past. Then ... *WHUMMMP!* and all went very dark indeed.

CHAPTER 5

Poor Weasel found himself under the snow yet again. It was getting to be an annoying sort of habit! But weirdly, it wasn't all that bad. At least he got a bit of peace and quiet for a change. But the silence was soon broken by a scrambled digging from above ... The next moment he found himself being hauled out into the fresh woodland air and plonked next to a rather stunned and shivery Doorkins.

'Ahhh,' Weasel said, smiling thankfully at their rescuers – Mole, Steadfast and her beetles. 'Good going, my friends!'

'All in a day's work, SIR!' The special ops officer gave a quick salute.

'Where's that moody white ermine?' one of the beetle crew asked. They called him 'Trusty Magoo' and he was quite the biggest beetle Weasel had ever seen. 'She's a bit shady if you ask me.'

'Well, no one is asking you, Private Magoo,' said Steadfast firmly.

Magoo snapped to attention, a little red-faced. The two other beetles sniggered.

'The ermine saved our furry hides just then,' claimed Weasel.

'Yes, I have to admit that was some jolly quick spy-like thinking,' agreed Mole thoughtfully.

Weasel picked up a long stick and began to prod the snow urgently, calling, 'OH, MISS ERMINE, MISS ERMINE, WHERE ARE YOU?'

The others glanced at each other, grabbed more sticks and joined in.

'AHEM!' a voice came from above. The frantically prodding animals looked up.

There, on a high snow-topped branch, was the sleek white ermine, flashing her amused and tilted smirk.

'The name's Blanche, Woodland Ranger Blanche.' She flipped down from the tree, landing lightly on the crisp snow.

A Woodland Ranger, thought Weasel admiringly. They were real tough cookies.

'Thank you for that daring rescue, er ... Blanche,' Weasel said, offering a paw. After a moment's hesitation, Blanche shook it with a cool nod.

CHOR, CHOR! CHOR, CHOR!

'Here comes Postie Phil,' said Weasel, pricking up his ears.

'PHIIIIIIIL!' he called extremely loudly.

There was no answer.

'PHIIIIIIIL!' he yelled again.

Still no answer.

Doorkins winced, his dormouse ears trembling. 'I don't think he can hear you, Weas—'

'PHIIIIIIIIL!' Weasel bellowed once more.

To the dormouse's relief, Postie Phil and Viv burst into the clearing panting heavily.

'So s-s-sorry, everyone, I messed up b-big style!' squawked Phil. Pheasants were a nervous lot, and would jump at a settling snowflake. Unfortunately Phil was more nervous than most.

Mole sat him down on a log and Doorkins produced a flask of his chocolatiest hot chocolate ever. The pheasant gratefully sipped the delicious drink to calm his flapping.

'What's occurring then, Phil?' asked Weasel gently.

'I-I was on my way to Beaver Lodge w-w-with a message for you, Weasel.' Phil pulled out a black envelope from his postie bag and handed it to the surprised super-agent with a shaky wing.

On the front in spidery writing, it read 'Agent Weasel, Beaver Lodge', and was stamped with a large glittery snowflake – charming, but also a little creepy.

'As I got near Bentbark Ridge,' Phil continued with a deep shuddering breath, 'I stopped to warm me toes for a minute. Suddenly, a huge scary shadow passed overhead. Well, I nearly jumped out of my feathers I can tell you. It chased me up the ridge and I actually had to FLY at one point!' His eyes widened at the thought.

A pheasant using its wings? It must have been squeaky-bottom-time and no doubt, thought Weasel.

'And that's when I er … met you guys.'

Weasel nodded, thinking it over as the other animals consoled the quivering bird. He looked down at the spooky envelope and ripped it open with his claw. Sparkly glitter and stars fell to the snow by his paws. 'Hmmm, nice touch,' muttered Weasel.

He pulled out a note scrawled with the same spidery letters. It read 'STAY AWAY!'

Er … stay away from what? he pondered. It didn't seem a particularly friendly kind of message. He noticed Blanche peeking over his shoulder and stuffed the note up his WI6 jumper out of sight. He would need to keep an eye on this Woodland Ranger. What was she up to?

'All ready for a jaunty little walk?' boomed Mole in a rather determined manner. She was keen to get on with the journey.

With the pedal sled well and truly buried and the daylight going fast, they had no choice but to continue on paw to Beaver Lodge.

'I'd feel safer joining you lot, b-but I've got loads more stuff to d-deliver,' trembled the poor postie pheasant. 'I just don't know if my nerves can take it!'

'Stick to the brambles and the undergrowth and you'll be tickety-boo,' suggested Weasel, patting the poor bird's back.

Phil straightened himself up and said his goodbyes. He dashed off into the woods with a *CHOR, CHOR* as he went.

'Take care, my feathery friend,' Weasel called as the pheasant disappeared between the frost-glittered trees.

'OOOOOOH!' groaned Viv hopelessly. 'I'm starving and my paws feel like blocks of ice.'

'Come on, Viv, chipper up, it's not far,' encouraged Weasel.

The bulky fox was definitely out of sorts – she was like a different animal. When they reached their cosy destination, Weasel would have a word about her whinging. Keeping up morale was an important job as team captain.

Dragging what they could of their scattered luggage, the animals began their difficult trek towards Beaver Lodge. Weasel just hoped they would have some energy left for the Winter Whopper Games tomorrow!

CHAPTER 6

As the group of weary animals reached the end of Bentbark Ridge, they looked down on a very welcome sight indeed.

Nestled at the end of a very frozen Reed Rush Pond stood Beaver Lodge. It looked like a pretty ordinary heap of twigs and branches at first glance, but it was far from that. A warm twinkly light spilled from the small windows and a thread of grey smoke twirled from a stubby chimneypot. It was just how Weasel remembered.

'Heeello, me dears,' came a cheerful voice from behind the group. There stood kindly Mother Beaver, to Weasel's great delight. She had a friendly glint in her beady black eyes and carried a big pile of logs – for the fire, he presumed.

'Give old Mother Beaver a big hug then?' she said, dumping the logs into Agent Mole's arms.

'Crikey, steady on!' Mole complained, staggering under the weight.

Mother Beaver waddled over to Weasel and wrapped him in the most major of bear-hugs. He could barely breathe as the air rapidly left his lungs. *SUFFERING STRANGLE WEED, I wouldn't like to get in a paw wrestle with her!* he thought as she eventually released her grip.

'Come on, young 'uns, let's get you in the warm. Father Beaver will be pleased as blackberry punch to see you all.'

Perked up by the hearty welcome and the idea of warmth and food, the animals practically skipped across the snow towards the homely lodge.

But Viv was some way behind, dragging her paws and grumbling. Muriel decided to flutter back over and chivvy her on.

What on earth has got into her? Weasel usually found Viv so light-hearted. Mind you, it had been a tricky old day, so he would let her off the hook this time.

As they bundled in through the little wooden door, the animals were hit by a blast of warm air and a wonderful niff. Dried herbs of every kind hung in bunches from the low ceiling and a toasty fire crackled in the hearth. Father Beaver crouched by an open oven as he pulled out a very large and delicious-looking pie.

'Well, if it isn't Agent Weasel himself, back at good old Beaver Lodge,' cried Father Beaver heartily. He whacked the oven door shut with his big flipper-like tail. *CLUNK!*

'Supper's nearly ready – make yourselves at home, everyone.'

Tummies began to rumble at the thought of digging into that scrumptious pie. Weasel turned, ready to drag the luggage in from the cold, but saw Mother Beaver plonking the last trunk down on the lodge floor with ease.

'Don't want you alpine athletes tweaking your backs or anything,' she said with a cheeky little wink. 'Say hello to our other guest – only arrived an hour ago.' She nodded to the far side of the lodge, where a hulking great form sat in the shadows hunched behind a large book called *The WI6 Big Book of Spying*.

HA! A fellow agent, thought Weasel as he strolled up, holding out a paw.

'Dear chap, so nice to meet you. I'm … YIKES!' he screeched as the book lowered.

'WEASEL!' cried a surprised but delighted voice.

'VIV?' Agent Weasel gawped at the large fox sat before him. 'B-But how did you ... ?'

BASH! The lodge door flew open as er ... *Viv?* stomped in, Muriel fluttering alongside her.

'I SMELL SOMETHING YUMMY!' Viv boomed, inhaling a deep whiff of Father Beaver's pie. Everybody looked from one fox to the other, like spectators at a shuttlebop match.

'WHAT?' Viv shrugged her shoulders as she looked around at the startled animals. She spotted the other Viv sat in the corner, glaring angrily. 'GULP! Erm … I AM VIV! W-WHO IS THIS IMPOSTER?' she howled, pointing an accusing paw at the other fox.

'WHY, YOU BIG CHEESY FLEABAG, YOU NICKED MY BEST JUMPER!' growled the other Viv. She slammed her spy book down on the table. *WHAMMM!*

'EEEEK!' yelped the first Viv. She turned, bolting straight out of Beaver Lodge and into the fading light.

'Viv, come back! There's mushroom and truffle pie!' called Doorkins hopefully.

But she had already disappeared into the pine trees beyond the clearing. Steadfast and her squad buzzed out of the door in quick pursuit.

'That,' said Blanche, 'was not Viv!'

Everybody looked at her, a little confused – apart from Weasel, who twizzled his whiskers thoughtfully.

'HEY! I'm the real Viv!' barked the … er … other Viv.

'Well, if you're Viv, who's that Viv?' said Mole, pointing out of the lodge door.

'That Viv,' said Weasel, arching his eyebrow knowingly, 'is Viv's twin brother ... Vic!'

There was a gasp of surprise. It had all clicked into place. The whining and general moodiness was most unlike the real Viv. Her brother, on the other paw, could be a particularly grouchy old thing. And he was the spitting image of his sister – other than the differing names on their scruffy jumpers.

'How in FAIRY FOXTAIL'S KNOLL did you end up here?' Weasel asked the huge fox.

Viv explained. She had bounced out of bed bright-eyed and bushy-tailed that morning, only to fall face down on the bedroom floor with a *THUMP!*

Hmmm, I know that feeling, thought Weasel.

To Viv's utter astonishment, both sets of

her paws had been tightly bound with bramble briars. After a long and very prickly operation, she managed to gnaw herself free.

She quickly gathered her stuff and she scampered off through the woods to Little Thicket Corner, the pick-up point for the Team United Woodlands sled. But it had already gone – and she found a set of fresh sled tracks disappearing over the frozen Babble Brook. Desperate to be at this year's Winter Whopper Games, Viv dashed to Hedgequarters for help. The Boffin Bunnies took some convincing, but eventually let her whizz off in the spare WI6 pedal sled. She took a shortcut to Beaver Lodge cross-country, avoiding the precarious Bentbark Ridge.

'You have a pedal sled HERE?' Weasel said excitedly, gripping Viv by her beefy shoulders.

'Yes. It's parked round the back, of course.'

'You are a GENIUS!' Weasel patted her warmly on the back. 'We'll be at Windtop Hill in no time tomorrow thanks to you.'

Viv beamed. Any praise from the WI6 super-spy made her grin like a buffoon. And it wasn't every day you got called a genius. If ever, in Viv's case.

'Do you think Vic's working for the other side?' asked Blanche in a serious tone.

'NAAAAH!' Viv chimed in. 'He's not clever enough for that. All he's interested in is food!'

As well as its reputation for sporting excellence, the games were known for an abundance of tasty grub – a major attraction for a fox like Vic.

'Er … what other side?' asked Mole, stiffening with worry.

'Oh! There's a new bunch of wrongdoers causing bother at the games!' Blanche replied, inspecting her claws matter-of-factly. 'Random snowball attacks, ice sculptures smashed, hot chocolate supplies pilfered ... I could go on.'

'OH NO!' gasped the others. The games could grind to a halt without its precious hot chocolate reserves.

'And that's not all,' she added, stony-faced now. 'A number of top athletes have disappeared ... never to be seen again!'

The animals didn't know what was more upsetting – the stolen hot chocolate or the missing competitors. It was shocking indeed!

'Who do they think's behind it?' asked Doorkins, nervously twiddling his paws.

Blanche seemed to turn whiter than a white ermine could possibly go.

'A name has been mentioned,' she said with a slight tremor to her voice.

'Come on, girl, spit it out!' said Mole.

'Well ...' Blanche said, stalling, 'it's the ... the ... the ABOMINABLE DR SNOW!'

There was deadly silence. You could hear a pine-needle drop. Even the beavers stopped what they were doing.

'Who's the Abob-nipple ... the Abom-nettle ... Who's this ... er ... Dr Snow?' asked Viv, looking around a little anxiously at the other animals.

The Abominable Dr Snow was only the most feared animal mega-villain ... like ever. Nobody knew who or what he was. But safe to say, the doctor was a bit of a NAUGHTY one all right.

'My job,' sighed Blanche, 'is to catch

whoever's behind this mischief and halt their abominable plans! *And* to win as many medals as possible for Team United Woodlands, of course.'

'Well, we shall help you, Ranger Blanche!' cried Weasel dramatically. 'After all, we are a team. TEAM UNITED WOODLANDS.'

'WOOD-LANDS, WOOD-LANDS, WOOD-LANDS,' the animals chanted together.

'Come on, everyone, grub's up,' bellowed Father Beaver. 'After a big feed and a good night's sleep, you'll be ready for anything tomorrow. Even tackling nasty super-villains!'

Doorkins looked out of the door towards the distant line of trees – there was no sign of Vic or the plucky beetles!

CHAPTER 7

Viv's snoring shook Beaver Lodge with a vengeance that night. It was a surprise that all the branches and twigs didn't shake off the roof. Even with two pillows stuffed over his head, Weasel struggled to get a wink of sleep.

But he'd been tossing and turning all night anyway, worrying about the missing fox twin.

Steadfast and her beetle crew had turned in late last night, tired and cold. Vic's paw prints had just vanished in the snow. The only thing they had found was a large white feather – quite unusual with black speckles around the edge. Maybe a clue, maybe not. But one thing was for sure: Vic had completely disappeared.

STRANGE FEATHER

Viv didn't seem particularly worried about her brother – he was big enough and ugly enough to look after himself. She guessed he was probably back at the den, safe and sound, scoffing something sugary from the larder. Weasel was inclined to agree, but there would be no harm in searching for the lumbering fox on their way up to Windtop Hill.

After a speedy breakfast of wild oat and blueberry pancakes – a delicious Father Beaver specialty – the animals were ready for the off.

Mother Beaver had, rather impressively for

such an elderly creature, lugged all the baggage on to the back of pedal sled two – plus a large hamper of packed lunch for the trip.

With three cheers for the beavers, the sled sped off in a puff of snow. Next stop the Winter Whopper Games!

The journey to Windtop Hill was fairly uneventful. If you call uneventful …

Losing the packed lunch off the back of the sled.

Losing Doorkins off the back of the sled.

Crashing into a buried tree stump and losing everybody off the back of the sled – except Blanche, who managed to hang on with her super Woodland Ranger skills.

It was starting to feel like a bad luck kind of trip.

There had been no sign of Vic. Weasel hoped to HIGH CONKERS that he was back at home reflecting on his poor behaviour – and that their luck would begin to change for the best.

The track got steeper and the animals sensed they were getting nearer, causing much excited twittering.

Blanche and Viv, who were now in the driving seat, strained with all their might up the incline. Then, to their utter relief, the

overloaded sled popped over the ridge with a
THUNK!

And there it was!

Towering into the ice-blue sky was the magnificent WINDTOP HILL.

'WHOAAA!' gasped Viv, her tongue lolling with astonishment.

'It's just a hill,' said Agent Mole, who was more impressed by underground stuff really.

'LOOK, DEEPDIP STADIUM!' Weasel pointed at the twinkling lights in the distance.

The stadium was freshly carved from ice and snow every two years, so it never looked the same twice! It was almost too far away to see, but it appeared to have a curvy swoosh thing going on this year. It would be the location of the opening ceremony that very night. Weasel could not wait!

As the sled passed through the twin-pine gates at the entrance to the Winter Whopper Games site, a voice called, 'OI, NOT SO FAST, YOU LOT!'

The animals had been completely fixed on the dramatic view in front of them and had failed to notice a little booth hollowed out in the pine tree trunk. Viv pulled on the air brakes and skidded to a stop.

DEEP DIP

A red squirrel frowned from beneath a large peaked cap, marched out and halted in front of the stationary sled. Squinting at a clipboard, she tutted and grumbled while scribbling away with a stubby pencil.

'I am Inspection Officer Scarlet,' she stated, eventually looking up. 'I will need to inspect this here vehicle before you proceed.'

Agent Weasel barely had a chance to reply before Officer Scarlet leapt on to the sled. She quickly scampered all over the luggage, peeking in every nook and cranny, lifting lids and sniffing loudly.

'Hmmmm, all seems to be in order,' she said. 'Apart from THIS!' She held up a small tin with 'Dr Pops' on the front.

Muriel fluttered to the top of the inspector's cap, eyeing up her tasty-looking wool scarf.

'Er ... those are chocolate sprinkles,' Doorkins said, shrugging.

'And what will these here ... *chocolate sprinkles* be used for?' asked the squirrel sternly as she popped off the lid and sniffed the contents.

The animals looked at each other, puzzled. 'HOT CHOCOLATE,' they all said at exactly the same moment.

'These here sprinkles look a bit dodgy to me,' she chittered, raising her eyebrows. 'There are no performance-enhancing potions allowed at the Games!' With that, she stomped off, taking the tin with her – while waving them on at the same time.

'How very dare you—!' began Weasel.

Blanche pedalled on, cutting him short. It wasn't a good idea to get on the wrong side of officials before the games had even started.

Weasel sighed heavily as Muriel plopped back on his shoulder, munching a rather large mouthful of something woolly. It was much the same colour as Inspection Officer Scarlet's scarf. He chuckled to himself and patted her little mothy head. *Good old Muriel.*

At last the sled pulled into Deepdip village and Weasel hopped down. There was so much activity, it was hard to know where to fix his peepers.

Deepdip was the nerve centre of the games

and definitely the place to be. Woodland animals from far and wide bustled around. Some relaxed drinking hot chocolate or sharing a sugary pine-syrup fondue. Others unloaded sleds or dashed here and there on ice-slide scooters.

'Ah, it's good to be back!' declared Weasel, stretching his back and rubbing his frozen paws together.

He turned to share his delight with the rest of the team ...

But everyone had completely vanished.

'Well I never!' he said.

Then he noticed the letter Phil Postie had given him, lying on the crisp snow. It must have fallen from his pullover as he jumped from the pedal sled. Weasel bent down to pick it up ... but hang on – this letter hadn't been opened. It must be a new one. He looked round suspiciously before quickly ripping it open. It read:

WATCH YOUR BACK, OR ELSE!

☺ 👍

CHAPTER 8

The threatening note set Weasel on edge. He was less worried about his own back and more about his absent teammates. Surely they hadn't gone far. He scanned the village square. Where in SHIVERING SNOW-CHOOKS had they got to?

To Weasel's relief, he saw Viv inspecting one of the food stalls. These were very strange tufty little kiosks, woven from what appeared to be dry mountain grass. This particular one displayed a fine array of fancy cakes. Viv gawped with wide hungry eyes, drooling at the sight.

Steadfast and her beetles were gathered round a small pine tree stump. Trusty Magoo sat locked in a paw wrestle with a large and mean-looking badger while the others cheered him on enthusiastically. *Soldiers will be soldiers*, thought Weasel.

Then he spotted Mole and Blanche. The pair were deep in conversation with a small vole wearing a bright green knitted bib with the title 'WHOPPER MAKER' on the front.

Ahhhh! This was one of the games' helpers. They were extremely friendly and very, very polite – sometimes annoyingly so.

The vole pointed to a large impressive slab of rock protruding from the snow at the other side of the square. Many animals pootled in and out of a low opening at the bottom as giant icicles hung from a stone ledge above, glinting in the sunlight.

This was the Winter Whopper Committee Headquarters, Weasel realised. It was a decidedly awesome sight.

A commotion off to the left caught Weasel's eye. It was Doorkins and Muriel. *Phew!* At least that was everyone accounted for.

Doorkins bounded frantically after the fluttering moth, who had a strand of bright green wool dangling from her mouth.

OH NO! The little vole's bib. It had unravelled so quickly that it now just read 'WHOPPER' on the front. Weasel hurtled over, zipping niftily between animals. With a mighty leap, he plucked the naughty moth right out of the air and landed back on the soft snow with a *FLUMP!* He whipped out a small wooden box from his pullover and popped the fuming moth inside.

'Cool off, Muriel,' he whispered through the air holes in the lid before stuffing it back up his WI6 spy jumper.

'Phew!' Weasel wiped his brow as the jolly vole toddled off, eager to help another lost or clueless creature. He was completely unaware he trailed a brand new and exceedingly long green tail!

'Th-thanks, old chum,' said a rather flustered

and red-faced Doorkins, then added, 'Er …
what's this?' He picked up a black envelope
that was lying on the snow. 'It looks like the
letter Postie Phil gave you yesterday – it must
have fallen out of your jumper.'

Weasel shuddered. It was another new,
unopened note. What was going on? He swept
the crowd of bustling animals, his spy-senses
tingling. Who had placed it there – right under
his snout?

'Are you all right, Weasel?' asked the
concerned dormouse.

'Er, yes, I'm fine, my friend. Just this chilly
wind giving me the shivers.'

But then Weasel spotted a tall dark figure
leaning against a roast chestnut stall. It wore
a long grey mack and a wide floppy hat that
drooped down to cover the character's face.

The creature casually rolled up a copy of the *Daily Conker* newspaper and strolled off towards the Winter Whopper Committee Headquarters with an unusual hoppy sort of limp.

Hmmm, curious, Weasel pondered, twizzling a whisker.

He tore open the envelope and read the note:

YOU HAVE BEEN WARNED.
☺ 👍 XX

Hmmm, that doesn't really explain much, does it! thought Weasel. Doorkins looked up at him expectantly.

'Ah! Just Granny Weasel – wondering when I'll be round for supper on our return,' Weasel said, shoving yet another letter up his jumper.

The rest of Team United Woodlands sauntered up to join them.

Viv sported a fine sugar-cream moustache. She'd obviously given in and scoffed some of those splendid-looking cakes after all.

Trusty dragged a large jar of pickled walnuts on a rickety old sledge. He must have won the paw wrestle with the fierce badger. By the smile on his face, he thought it was a fine prize. But the walnuts reminded Weasel of squishy little brains ... double yuck!

Agent Mole walked up with Blanche. 'We must go and register NOW at the Winter Whopper Headquarters.' She waved tiredly at the large stone slab across the square.

The effects of the sleepless night were clearly taking their toll. The team needed a really good kip before the opening ceremony of the games that evening – apart from Viv, who had slept very well last night, thank you very much. She was ready to party.

The gaggle of animals reluctantly trudged off towards the Committee Headquarters. An assortment of delicious smells hit them as they tramped across the square. Sugared acorns on sticks, sap-syrup toffee apples, cheese-nettle melts ... it went on.

It was all too much for the poor famished creatures, who'd lost their packed lunch from the sled earlier that day!

'I am so hungry, I might just pass out!' said Viv, putting a paw to her forehead.

She had, in fact, just gorged herself at the

fancy cake stall minutes before. The sugar-icing evidence was all around her chops. Weasel silently chuckled – it clearly took a lot of nosh to fill up a fox that size.

It was quite a shock to walk into the games committee building, such a huge and cavernous space. A large crack in the ceiling flooded the cave with orangey light from the low sun.

A long queue of impatient-looking animals shuffled towards a shiny quartz desk at the far end. The wall behind displayed the triple fir-cone emblem of the Winter Whopper Games.

'Wowee … look at these statues!' said Viv in awe.

Ice sculptures of past champions stood in arched nooks around the walls.

'Er … shall we get in that queue?' said

Blanche nervously. 'We don't want to miss our … er … registration!' The white ermine seemed less cool, calm and collected than usual.

'Hang on, doesn't that statue remind you of anyone?' asked Doorkins, pointing a paw at an ice sculpture a couple of nooks from where they stood.

'B-But it's … it's … BLANCHE!' blurted Viv.

CHAPTER 9

There was no doubt – the statue was Blanche all right ... or a very, very close relative. It was confirmed by the plaque on the plinth, which read:

WOODLAND RANGER BLANCHE, WINTER WHOPPER ICE-BOOGIE CHAMPION – Team Northern Forest

Ice-Boogie involved skilfully sliding round on an ice-covered pond while throwing some seriously funky moves to dance music. It was very popular and particularly excellent to watch.

'BUT, BLANCHE, we had no idea!' cried Weasel.

Blanche inspected the floor, looking a little embarrassed.

'Not the obvious sport for a hardened Woodland Ranger though, is it?' she said, her cheeks pink.

'But, Blanche, I LOOOOVE ICE-BOOGIE!' Weasel bellowed. All the other team members nodded in agreement. It was one of the Whopper's best events. Blanche smiled properly for the first time since they'd all met.

'Ahem!' said a wee but firm voice. A chunky brown bird looked at them over the top of her round-rimmed spectacles. She had a rather snooty expression on her beak. 'I am Gerit Grouse, Whopper Committee clerk. YOU, I presume, are Team United Woodlands? You are the LAST team to register. Can you come with me please – quickly!'

She waddled off towards the shiny quartz desk. Agent Weasel shrugged and they all followed.

The other animals stuck in the long queue for tickets began to grumble.

'OI, NO QUEUE-JUMPING, YOU BOG-SNUFFLERS!' This was the big paw-wrestling badger, still feeling upset after losing his pickled walnuts, no doubt.

Gerit Grouse turned on the spot. She tottered up to the badger and said very firmly, 'Back of the line please!'

'B-B-BUT …' blurted the badger.

Gerit pointed to the end of the line. The badger could see she meant it and sloped off, looking rather sorry for himself. This was a bird not to be messed with, Weasel decided.

The little brown grouse suddenly bobbed up from behind the desk, thumping down a big pile of paper in front of Agent Weasel – the rather sizeable registration document which all teams had to sign.

'I need a signature from your captain – here, here, here aaaaaand here please,' she said, flapping a wing at the topmost sheet.

The other animals looked on eagerly, as Weasel scribbled his name with the scratchy feather-quill pen.

I could be signing away my precious acorn collection for all I know, he thought. But there was a bit of a rush on, them being the last team to register, so he just did as he was told.

Gerit tweaked her glasses and inspected the form. 'Very good – now your team coach please.'

'COACH?' gawped Weasel, baffled.

'Yes, it's the new rules. No coach, no Winter Whopper!' she said matter-of-factly, sipping from a small cup of frothy hot chocolate.

Agent Weasel could not stand rules and regulations.

It drove his boss H, head-honcho hedgehog at WI6, completely bonkers. She liked everything done by the book – rules were there to be followed. But not for Weasel. Not on your NELLY!

PEEEEEEEEP
PEEEEEEP

PEEEEEEEEEEEP!

Everyone jumped out of their fur at the high-pitched din. Even Gerit Grouse looked a little out of sorts. 'I am the team coach!' declared Doorkins firmly. He was now sporting a red peaked cap and holding a clipboard, with a whistle dangling around his neck.

Weasel scratched his head. How odd. Had Doorkins been prepared for this all along? It certainly seemed that way. Only, Weasel knew how flustered his best pal could get with leadership stuff. Ah well, if it got them into the games, then so be it.

'HOORAY FOR COACH DOORKINS!' cried Viv.

'HOORAY FOR COACH DOORKINS!' the others joined in.

The little dormouse grinned from ear to ear.

After the signing was complete, it was team photo time.

The photographer shuffled in under a large black blanket, with a rather wobbly old box-camera set on a tripod. Impatiently, he waved them to move a step backwards. The team shuffled towards the wall.

'Watch the birdie,' croaked the photographer in a high scratchy voice. There was a FLASH and a puff of grey smoke. The animals blinked, a little dazed from the glare. Then ... *CRACK! CREEEEEEEEEK!*

'LOOK OUT!' cried Weasel as he swung round to see a huge sculpture tipping from the nook behind them. He barged Team United

Woodlands out of harm's way, only to slip flat on his face on a chunk of ice.

EEK! I'm going to be smushed!

The statue must have stopped centimetres from the super-agent's head. He looked up to see Steadfast and the beetles straining to hold the giant icy lump, with Trusty Magoo taking most of the weight.

To everyone's shock, stood in the nook, her eyes wide and wings outstretched, was Gerit Grouse. She looked to be in some kind of trance – surely this wasn't the same bird!

'GO, WEASEL, GO!' bellowed Trusty, his legs trembling with the load.

Weasel looked up. The photographer was making a run for it.

COBBLY COBNUTS – it was that dodgy fellow in the mack and floppy hat. Weasel could feel a red mist coming on – the Weasel War Dance. Uh-oh!

It usually occurred when a weasel was in a fix and its fury took over. Sure enough, Weasel flipped into the air with an agile spin, landing on all fours … and then the wild bottom shaking began.

OOOOOSH

Weasel needed to keep control. It could send him completely bonkers.

He sprang to his feet, feeling the War Dance power, and belted straight after the shifty character. Blanche followed close behind.

The villain bashed through queuing animals at high speed, sending the poor moody badger flying on to the hard stone floor with a *THWUMP.*

OOOHHH, he groaned. It really wasn't his day.

The shady-mack critter hopped and zig-zagged at astonishing speed, chased by Weasel and Blanche. The three animals zipped out of the building and into the open square.

Scooting between the food kiosks, the scoundrel made a sudden and incredible leap over the stall ahead. Weasel had never seen anything like it.

WHUMP! Weasel went straight through the stall, bursting out the other side – covered in bright pink candy floss. *Yum*, he thought, nibbling as he sprinted on.

Blanche raced past Weasel on an ice-slide scooter. 'SORRY, IMPORTANT WI6 BUSINESS, MA'AM!' she shouted back to a very astonished Whopper Maker squirrel – as if that made up for pinching it.

Crossing the crowded snow slopes, the shady figure sped towards a group of barkboard students taking a lesson. The ne'er-do-well clattered through – *BOSH!* – and the poor animals tumbled like a set of dominoes.

Blanche swerved to avoid the chaos and hit a rather large jump-ramp. *SWOOOSH!* She launched into the air and – *THUNK!* – she somehow lodged herself in the nearest fir tree.

'GO, WEASEL, GO!' she cried, hanging upside-down by the tips of her paws.

Weasel grabbed a barkboard from a rather stunned young field mouse and yelled, 'SORRY, IMPORTANT WI6 BUSINESS, YOUNG SIR!'

Well, if Blanche could do it, so could he.

Running at full pelt, he dropped the board on to the snow and skilfully hopped on. With the War Dance power flowing through his veins, Weasel began to gain on shady-mack.

He raced across the slope as a gaggle of rowdy geese flew over the ridge, sliding on inflatable rings. *SWOOSH, SWOOSH, SWOOSH.*

They honked in thrilled delight. One brushed the tops of Weasel's ears as it sailed over. *PHEW! That was close*, he thought.

Shady-mack was heading for the Pumpkin Lift. Making a super-animal leap, the villain grabbed on to a car dangling high above the snow. Weasel dug in for a hard turn and hurtled towards a big freestyle ramp.

A bunch of young rabbits dived for cover as he hit the jump. *Plop, plop, plop* – they went headfirst into the snowdrifts either side.

WHOOOOSH! The W16 super-spy soared

through the air, just catching his foe's long white furry feet. The animals in the car above peeked out nervously at the grappling pair, causing the Pumpkin Lift to swing rather precariously.

Shady-mack managed to free a long white foot and – *CLUMP!* – bashed poor Weasel hard on the head.

Weasel's paws jolted free and he fell towards the ground.

As he looked up his opponent, still dangling from the disappearing car, gave an annoying little wave.

Then ... *BOING, BOING, BOING!* Weasel found an unexpectedly soft and bouncy landing.

He had flopped on top of a large inflatable ring! Ranger Blanche had shoved it under the plummeting agent, saving his hide yet again.

'Don't want our captain splatted on the first

day!' she said with a
relieved look.

*Wow, what
an animal*, Weasel
thought. She really was
becoming part of the
team. He was about to
give his thanks when …

'AHEM!'

Both looked round.

Uh-oh! They were
in real trouble now.

It was H, head-
honcho hedgehog at
WI6. She sat in her sled
with two enormous badger
bodyguards. And she did not look best pleased!
In fact she looked darn right cross.

109

CHAPTER 10

The WI6 chief took off her specs, sighed deeply and began to polish the lenses on her silk necktie – a pretty good sign that she was annoyed. Very annoyed indeed!

'Good day, Agent Weasel,' she said rather haughtily, 'nice to see you up to your usual tricks again.' She waved a paw at the path of destruction – leading all the way back to the Winter Whopper Committee

Headquarters. 'NOT very by the book, I must say!'

Blanche opened her mouth to explain, but H held up a paw.

'I expected better from you, Woodland Ranger Blanche. You came highly recommended for this mission.' She looked down her snout at the surprised white ermine. 'Just remember, just because you have relatives in high places –' by this she meant Blanche's distant cousin, Principal Pine Marten – 'doesn't mean I can't put a black mark or two on your record!'

'Now look here, H,' said Weasel, getting quite annoyed himself now.

H abruptly cut him off. 'If the Abominable Dr Snow is behind this mayhem, I don't care how cold it is around here – things are going to get pretty hot, believe me.' She wagged a paw at the two stunned animals. 'Your mission is to find whoever this rascal is and put a stop to his dastardly deeds. Or we'll have to put a stop to the Winter Whopper Games immediately. So pack in mucking about and get it solved!' With that, H and the sled swished off.

'Oh, and, Weasel!' H cried from the back of the sled. 'Do NOT be late for tonight's opening ceremony!'

'How very dare she – as if we'd be late!' Weasel said, completely exasperated.

Much later …

PEEP! PEEP! PEEP!

'WE'RE LATE! WE'RE LATE!' Doorkins scuttled around in a mad panic, blowing his whistle for all he was worth. The team had overslept.

When they'd arrived at the athletes' village, the mood had been a bit low – what with the roasting from H and the news that Flufftail Speedoffski of the Bunny Top-sliders and Half-loop McPaw of the Freestyle Ferrets had disappeared.

Not only that, but the five-star Freeze-Inn hotel was completely jam-packed and Team United Woodlands had to settle for the three-star Cosy Pine Tree apartments. Which, if Weasel was honest, sounded better than a night in a chilly freezer box – give him a toasty hole in a tree anytime.

But if anything, the apartment had been too cosy and the whole team had quickly fallen into a deep sleep.

THE
COSY PINE
TREE

PEEEEEEEP
PEEEEEEP

'IT'S
GOING TO START
ANY MINUTE!'
screeched
Doorkins at
the top of his
squeaky voice.
Was Doorkins already
struggling with the
pressure of being team
coach? It had only been
half a day. Weasel patted
his little buddy on the
shoulder for comfort. The
dormouse took a deep breath
and seemed to relax a bit.

'RIGHT, LET'S GO!' urged Mole, as keen as ever to be off.

The animals piled into the WI6 pedal sled and bombed over to Deepdip Stadium as fast as their spinning paws would carry them.

Drawing nearer, they saw it was completely chock-a-block. Even the surrounding pine trees shook with excited animals.

'Let's get up to Grand View Point,' suggested Weasel eagerly. 'One, it's a grand view, and two, there's no point in hanging around here!'

Off they went, pedalling for all they were worth up Windtop Hill.

The view from Grand View Point was spectacular – as you might expect. Sparkly lights and spotlight beams shimmered all around.

Blanche nudged Weasel, pointing to the VIP box. Sitting next to Principal Pine Marten was a very grumpy-looking H.

Oh dear! H had told them not to be late. And Team United Woodlands had missed the athletes' parade altogether. No wonder she looked a bit miffed!

'Shame we don't have any nibbles,' sighed Viv. To her delight, Coach Doorkins pulled out a big brown paper bag full of wild-wheat butter popcorn.

'YESSSS!' declared Viv, pumping her paw in the air. The team settled in for the show.

'LOOK!' cried Doorkins, pointing to a group of twinkly lights just above the treetops.

'Are those UFOs?' asked Mole, by which she meant 'Unidentified Flying Odd-things'.

'Noooo, of course not. That's the Firefly Aerial Display Team!' said Blanche excitedly.

'OOOOOOH, AAAAAAAH!' went the

crowd as the display team came to a halt, hovering over the stadium.

In a beam of light below, the Mountain Twang Band, a popular wood-pigeon combo, struck up a tune.

As they hit the first note, the fireflies burst into action. Awesome shapes appeared in the sky in perfect time to the music – snowflakes, butterflies, daisies, even a spectacular eagle. It was so realistic, some of the smaller animals ducked for cover. The insects then formed the triple fir-cone symbol of the Winter Whopper Games ... and with a final swoosh, exploded in a shower of light.

The crowd went wild!

'HOW ON EARTH ARE THEY GOING TO TOP THAT?' wondered Corporal Steadfast.

Unfortunately the next thing certainly didn't. A series of games officials proceeded to make some awfully long, boring speeches, mainly about how it wasn't the winning but the taking part that was important.

Yeah, right! everybody thought.

Half the audience were dozing off, until Principal Pine Marten stood up and announced, 'Animals and creatures, we are now about to witness something very special indeed.' She raised her paws high for dramatic effect. 'Claus Vonberg, wildcat snowdrift-jump supremo, will light the Ever-Burning Fir Cones –' she waved to the three cones mounted at the far end of the stadium – 'in a spectacular mid-air leap never seen before!'

An excited thrum went around the crowd.

A spotlight picked out Vonberg at the top

of a very, very big ice-slide jump. She clutched a burning torch in her claw, crouching and ready to go, looking particularly fierce and cool.

Well, this is more like it, thought Weasel, rubbing his paws together. Suddenly a large dark shadow passed just overhead. *SWOOSH!*

It dived headlong towards the stadium just as the fearless wildcat was about to begin her run. The shadow swooped, plucking Vonberg from the top of the ramp. And then … she was gone.

The burning torch rolled down the slope and plopped to the stadium floor.

Weasel gasped. His teammates gasped. The crowd gasped.

'YOU PESKY ANIMALS WERE WARNED! DID ANYONE ACTUALLY READ MY LETTERS?' said a rather hysterical croaky voice over the stadium tannoy. 'WELL, YOU'RE REALLY FOR IT NOW!'

Out of the gloom, a figure bounded from the public address hut and hopped across the ice.

'GET THAT ANIMAL!' screeched H, jumping from her seat.

A spotlight fixed on the mysterious creature. Of course, it was the one and only shadymack, still in the big coat and floppy hat. The figure bent down to pick up the burning torch.

Was that a fluffy white tail poking out of the back?

Weasel was the only one who seemed to notice. Then, to his horror, he spotted a barrel packed with rockets. It was right next to shady-mack, who now held ... A BURNING TORCH!

GULP! He had the feeling this was not going to end well. Those fireworks were for a celebration, not a disaster. But the scoundrel was pointing the biggest rocket at Grand View Point – straight up at Team United Woodlands!

WHOOOOOSH! went the massive firework as the wretch lit the fuse. The team hit the deck as the rocket screamed overhead.

Then ... *BOOOOM!*

The whole hill began to tremble.

'AVALANCHE!' cried Woodland Ranger Blanche.

BOOOOM!

CHAPTER 11

Shady-mack dropped through a hole in the stadium floor and disappeared. Weasel was fuming. It was just not on – that rotter was saving its own fur while everyone else was about to be smushed.

'I HAVE AN IDEA!' cried Blanche over the thundering roar of the avalanche. 'ON MY COUNT OF THREE, EVERYBODY JUMP.'

Viv looked puzzled – numbers were really not her thing. Even counting up to three made her nervous!

'Just jump when she says jump!' Weasel said reassuringly.

The rumble grew louder.

'READY?' yelled Blanche. 'ONE, TWO, THREE … JUUUUUUMP!'

There was a deafening *ROOOOOOAR* as they leapt. To their astonishment, Team United Woodlands were now riding the crest of a charging avalanche!

Well, this is a bit odd, thought Weasel.

As they rolled and tumbled towards the panic-filled stadium, a wood-panelled sign sped alongside them. It read:

DANGER AVALANCHE

It's a little bit late for that, mused Weasel.

But then he noticed this side of the stadium had a large swooping wall – and in the middle of the wall was a gate. If they could bash that gate open, most of the snow would whoosh straight through the opening and not over the fretting animals!

A light bulb pinged on in his super-agent brain.

In the blink of an eye, Weasel had flipped up on to the hurtling sign and proceeded to surf the giant wave of snow!

'EVERYBODY, GET ON!' he yelled, swishing across to his astonished teammates.

One by one they managed to roll or clamber on.

'YAAAAHOO!' whooped the beetles flying just overhead, loving every minute of this potential disaster.

'GRAB THAT TREE, VIV – WE'RE GOING TO RAM THE GATE!' cried Weasel.

Viv nodded and grabbed for a passing tree

trunk. She pointed it, jousting style, straight at the centre of the approaching gate!

'PREPARE FOR IMPACT!' yelled Weasel.

Everyone shut their eyes tight, apart from the beetles, who wanted to savour every single second!

There was an almighty *SMASH, CRASH, SWOOSH* as they hit the gate. The avalanche rumbled through like a fast-flowing river, eventually coming to a stop in the middle of the stadium floor.

A great cheer erupted from the relieved and grateful crowd.

Weasel sat up, a little dazed. He spotted various furry legs poking out from the deep snow.

'PHEW! Well, that was SNOW joke!' he said, in an attempt to lighten the mood.

'UUUUUGH!' groaned his buried colleagues.

After the brave WI6 team extracted themselves from the settled avalanche, Doorkins shuffled up and handed Weasel something.

'Take a look at this,' he said, passing Weasel a white feather.

Hmmm! he thought. It had the same black speckled markings as the one they'd found at Beaver Lodge.

'A flying menace, eh!' Weasel said, inspecting it. Could this have anything to do with Vic's disappearance? Weasel hoped not. He pictured Vic at home in front of a cosy fire, scoffing bucket loads of goose-gog-crumble and custard. Paws crossed that was where he was.

But another star of the games had been nabbed. This was turning into a right old pickle.

A loud and sudden *ROAAAAAR* from the crowd caused Weasel to nearly jump out of his WI6 spy pullover.

Someone had lit the Ever-Burning Fir Cones and the animals were going wild.

What do you know – it was Corporal Steadfast and the beetles! They hovered above the stadium, proudly holding the Winter Whopper torch aloft. Team United Woodlands jumped and cheered proudly.

'AHEM!' came a stiff voice over the tannoy and all became quiet. 'Animals and creatures, may I have your attention?' It was H, standing on the podium looking deadly serious. 'With tonight's attack, nearly half of our big-name competitors are missing. Hot chocolate supplies have been pilfered. And marshmallows and sprinkles are practically non-existent.'

There was a gasp from the crowd.

'As head of overall security, I have no choice but to postpone the twenty-first Winter Whopper Games. I thank you for your patience!' And with that, she stepped down.

The BOOS were deafening – particularly when two large badgers put out the Ever-Burning Fir Cones with leaky old watering cans.

Steadfast and the beetles looked utterly deflated.

As the rowdy and rather cross animals herded out of the stadium, Weasel felt a tap on the shoulder.

GULP! It was H and she was polishing her specs again!

'Agent Weasel. Team United Woodlands.'
She nodded curtly. 'I thank you for saving all
those innocent creatures this evening …'

Weasel could feel a great big 'BUT'
coming on.

'BUT this troublesome trickster escaped
you YET AGAIN! And another top athlete
is missing. WHAT do you have to say for
yourselves?'

The animals shifted uneasily.

'Well—' began Weasel, but H sharply cut
him off.

'We will meet at the Hot Choccie
Emporium at eight hundred hours in the
morning. And we will sort this lot out.' She
prodded a paw at Weasel's midriff – H was
a bit squat, even for a hedgehog. 'Do not be
late. And bring that lot with you. And …

er … that will be all!' She marched off, her beefy badgers in tow.

'How very rude,' said Weasel.

The next morning …

PEEP, PEEP, PEEP!

'Everybody up. Everybody up – QUICKLY!' bellowed Doorkins.

Oh no! Not late again, thought Weasel. He'd woken from a rather pleasant dream, where he'd won the barkboard downhill in record time. He'd been just about to receive his golden fir-cone medal when Doorkins started his peeping. *PEEP, PEEP, PEEP!*

Being late for the meeting with H was just not an option. Weasel leapt from his bed and *– CLUNK–CRASH–BOSH –* went straight over his hefty travel trunk again!

'FLYING FIDDLESTICKS,' he growled.

PEEP, PEEP, PEEP! went Doorkins's whistle. Weasel looked up from the floor and saw the cuckoo clock on the wall said five thirty. Way too early for the Hot Choccie Emporium – what was his buddy playing at?

Doorkins burst into the room wearing full coaching gear.

'TRAINING TIME! Games or no games!'

Hmmm! His mousey pal was taking this coaching lark way too seriously. Oh well, at least Weasel wasn't late for the meeting with H.

After a gruelling workout of log-lugging, slush-crawling, lung-busting slope-scurrying and a particularly chilly ice-dunk, the team were shattered. But the beetles kind of enjoyed it. It was just like army training all over again.

After a wash and brush-up, they trundled over to Deepdip village for the dreaded meeting with H.

The famous Hot Choccie Emporium served the best cup of HC in the whole of the United Woodlands – apart from Doorkins's chocolatiest hot chocolate ever, but that went without saying.

H sat outside. Her bulky bodyguards attempted to blend into the background – quite unsuccessfully from Weasel's point of view.

She sported a pair of fashionable sunglasses and woolly scarf almost bigger than she was. The cafe looked busy and had a jolly atmosphere, regardless of last night's chaos. H looked a bit out of place with the big frown across her brow.

'Good morning, H,' said Weasel cheerily.

'Agent Weasel. Team United Woodlands,' H greeted them with a frosty nod.

Really, it wasn't surprising H was in a grump. Most hedgehogs were generally tucked up asleep at this time of year. But she did not have the time to hibernate in a nice cosy woodpile – or anywhere else, for that matter.

She pulled a strained face at the racket a few tables down where a bunch of over-enthusiastic grey squirrels posed for a photograph.

POOOOF went the bright flash on the camera.

'I suppose we should get a round of hot chocolates?' H suggested.

She turned to wave over the first available waiter. *THWUMP!* A snowball hit H full in the face and knocked her out cold.

CHAPTER 12

The grey squirrels stood as rigid as pine trees, snowballs in their paws. A strange trance-like look was fixed on their faces. It reminded Weasel of Gerit Grouse when she'd tried to squish his team the day before.

And there, sloping off in the background, was shady-mack. Well, of course. He carried the very same rickety tripod camera he'd used at the Committee Headquarters.

Weasel tensed, ready to give chase. He could feel the red mist of his War Dance coming on again.

WHOOSH WHOOSH

'ATTACK!' shady-mack cried, then cowardly slipped away between the tables. The zombified squirrels seemed to be under his control and began pelting the WI6 team in a non-stop barrage. H's bodyguards could not get near her – still slumped unconscious across the table.

Viv, Mole and Blanche returned fire. The big fox had trained hard for the Snowball Dodge event, so her technique was pretty awesome and a couple of good strikes took a few of the squirrels out.

Meanwhile Steadfast and her squad dive-bombed the attackers – thwarting their

POFF POFF

snowball
throwing as much
as they could.

But poor
Doorkins,
still packing his first snowball,
took a large icy one right on the head.

Furious, Weasel's bottom shook as he leapt high into the air. The Weasel War Dance took over and he began to launch snowballs like a machine, laying out his foes left, right and centre. And a few unfortunate waiters to boot!

'WEASEL!' shrieked Doorkins. Two of the squirrel zombies had broken off from the rest and grabbed H's motionless body. Without even a flinch at the hedgehog spines, the furry felons sped off.

Weasel shook his head to clear the red mist and bolted straight after them.

'HEY! WAIT FOR ME!' cried Doorkins, jumping on to his chum's back as he flew past. Weasel didn't mind – he was glad to have his best buddy along for the ride.

The squirrels dashed straight for a group of animals patiently waiting for a red-kite air-lift to the top of Windtop Hill. The little critters wrenched barkboards and backpacks out of their paws without a thought.

'HEY!' yelled a ferret sporting a 'Whopper Maker' bib. 'That's just not on!'

To his astonishment, his board was unexpectedly whipped out of his paws by Agent Weasel.

'SORRY, SIR, IMPORTANT WI6 BUSINESS!' It was a bit naughty, but Weasel loved using that line sooooo much!

He hopped on the barkboard and raced down towards the Le Croc Sure cafe – the most expensive eatery in Deepdip village.

As the squirrels swooshed in through the open door, Weasel was right on their big bushy tails.

'LOOK OUT!' cried Doorkins.

A toad waiter leapt out of their way just in time, landing smack-bang in the middle of a large elderberry cream cake. *SPLAT!*

'SORREE,' called Doorkins, as they clattered into the breakfast lounge and food and customers flew everywhere.

The pair burst out on to the balcony, just as the squirrels dropped out of sight on to the snow beyond. Straight in front of Weasel, a party of well-to-do-looking animals were tucking into a big pot of shared fondue.

Weasel took emergency action and pop-jumped on to the cluttered table … *CLANK–CRASH–CRUNCH–SPLAT–SPLONK.*

SWOOSH! Weasel and Doorkins flew off the balcony edge and away. The gunk-splattered VIPs could only sit and gawp in stupefied shock.

Weasel looked down at his WI6-issue spy jumper, now covered in icky fondue juice.

'Ah, there goes another one, Doorkins!' he sighed. Weasel had a bad habit of ruining jumpers. *Oh well!* He had a few spares in his travel trunk, so no biggie.

'Mmmm, mumm, mumm!' replied Doorkins. Weasel looked round to see a rather large and buttery corncob stuck in his buddy's chops. The dormouse tugged it out and cried, 'WEASEL, THE TREES!'

The squirrels disappeared into the forest ahead, still carrying H. Agent Weasel crouched and flexed his knees to pick up speed. *WHOOSH!*

But their quarry had completely vanished. *Where on earth have the furry scoundrels got to*, thought Weasel as he darted the barkboard in between the tall upright pines.

'LOOK OUT,' squeaked Doorkins urgently.

The missing terrors crashed in from the left through some thick spruce branches.

Doorkins lobbed the corncob – *THUNK* – catching the nearest one right between the eyes. It had no effect whatsoever.

But Weasel and Doorkins had been barged off-course. They hit a snowdrift and were launched high into the air.

'YEEEOWWW!' yelled the little dormouse as the WI6 spy took them into a 360 spin. *THWUMP!* The duo landed safely back on the snow and burst from the trees.

The squirrels carved across the snow in tandem. They held on to H, who appeared to be completely out of it – she didn't even twitch a whisker.

'Er, Weasel?' began Doorkins politely.

Weasel didn't notice, only crouched into the turn and picked up speed.

'WEASEL?' the dormouse said a little more anxiously.

Weasel twisted round to look at his friend, a little miffed.

'I could be wrong, but I think we're about to ... GO OVER A CLIFFFFFFF!' Doorkins squealed at the top of his voice.

YICKERTY YIKES! A big yawning drop suddenly appeared before them. And to their absolute horror, the squirrels and H swooshed straight over the edge without a blink.

Weasel slammed his paws into the snow, squeezing his eyes shut. But the pair popped off the barkboard, sliding along on their tummies until they finally came to a stop ...

Weasel could feel a strong breeze blowing

up from the valley bottom. He carefully opened his eyes and gulped.

Doorkins dangled below, desperately gripping Weasel's rapidly stretching pullover sleeves. The dormouse looked over his shoulder and let out a little whine.

'Don't look down, my friend!' Weasel barked urgently. He was hanging upside-down by his paws from a small, crumbly ledge. Would it hold? And, CRIKEY, were they high up or what?

Weasel watched the blank-faced squirrels pop open a couple of parachutes from the pinched backpacks and float safely down towards the valley floor. It would have been a very different story if those packs had contained a few snacks and some thermal underwear! *Lucky, I guess*, thought Weasel.

As the parachutes drifted apart, the squirrels began to lose grip of their captive … until they let go altogether! H's limp body fell to the trees below.

'NOOOOOOOO!' cried Weasel.

A dark shadow whooshed straight overhead – it was a huge white snowy owl, diving for the plummeting hedgehog. Just as H was about to hit the treetops, it scooped her up in its massive talons. The owl turned briskly and clipped the descending squirrels as it flew back up, causing their parachutes to fold in. They plunged to a waiting snowdrift below … *FLOP, FLOP!*

With a powerful stroke of its wings, the immense bird soared back up at the intrepid duo, trailing H's long scarf below.

'Here goes nothing,' sighed Weasel as the owl swept above.

He stuck out a rear paw and made a grab for the dangling scarf. With a sizeable jolt, he and Doorkins were hauled into the ice-blue sky – up, up and away.

CHAPTER 13

The scarf flapped about like a flag in a gale, and Weasel found it increasingly difficult to keep hold. His little buddy clung on perilously to his pullover sleeves – now stretched to the max. It was a darn good job this was a WI6 jumper and not some other cheap rubbish, thought Weasel.

The monstrous bird glided upwards. Wherever it was taking them, Weasel hoped it wasn't too far!

'H,' he whispered, as loud as he dared. Owls had excellent hearing and he didn't want to end up as a mid-morning snack for this one. But it was no use – the head-honcho hedgehog was still out cold.

Doorkins nodded towards the ground below. They were passing over Deepdip. The village looked like a toy town full of scurrying ants. Were the other team members OK, Weasel wondered? The snowball fight had been pretty full on – he hoped they'd survived uninjured.

Without warning, the owl took a sharp turn towards the opposite side of Windtop Hill.

Locals called this the dark side. It was a lonely chilly place where the sun didn't shine and hardly anyone went – I mean, why would you? The thought of it sent a shudder down Weasel's spine.

As the bird rounded the peak, Weasel could

make out a black smudge on the lower slope. It soon became clear as they drew closer – this was no smudge, but an entrance to a deep dark cave.

The owl stilled its huge flapping wings and glided straight for the opening.

Weasel gulped. *We are not going to make it.*

'We're coming in too low!' whispered his dormouse chum in desperation.

Weasel scurried rapidly up the scarf by his rear paws. It was far from easy, particularly when you were upside-down, hauling your best buddy with you! But Doorkins still dangled too low.

He looked up with wide eyes at his super-spy pal. 'It's been nice knowing you, dear chap.'

There was no way Weasel would let this happen. Just as they were about to thump into the rock face, Weasel heaved Doorkins up by his jumper sleeves.

They bumped and skidded along the ground, dragged by the long scarf. It snagged on a prickly bush, instantly unravelling from H's shoulders.

SHWUMP! The pair slid to a halt in a crumpled heap.

The great owl swooped into the cave and disappeared.

'Well, my friend,' said Weasel, patting his buddy on the back. 'THAT ... could have been soooo much worse!'

Doorkins just raised his eyebrows in a 'DO YOU REALLY THINK SO' kind of way.

'Hey, look at this!' Doorkins picked up a fluffy white feather with black speckles around the edge.

'I thought as much, old chum,' said Agent Weasel. 'We follow that bird and we find our villain.'

'And get H back?' prompted the small mouse.

'Oh y-yes, absolutely,' he replied, a little vaguely. 'Right, let's be off.' And he marched into the cave.

'Er … Weasel, isn't it a little dark in there?' said Doorkins nervously.

Weasel stopped and nodded his head, thinking. 'Ah, yes! I have just the thing, my friend.' He rummaged round in his WI6 spy jumper and pulled out a large … peppermill.

Doorkins looked a tad unsure. Weasel rotated the top, in the hope that a light beam might appear out of the end. 'AAAACHOOO!' he sneezed. No, just pepper. He rummaged again.

Ah-ha! Weasel now held a small tin lantern.

'Er … any matches, old chap?' asked Weasel awkwardly. Luckily Doorkins always kept some in his little leather bag for such an emergency.

Once the small lantern was lit, the comrades cautiously made their way into the gloomy cave.

In the dim flickering light, creepy shadows leapt about the rough stone walls. Huge icy stalactites, hanging down from the high ceiling, didn't help much. Doorkins saw crouching monsters and spooky ghouls behind every rock.

At least there was no sign of that big snowy

owl – just the odd white speckled feather on the frost-covered ground. But Weasel was sure they'd bump into the big hulking bird soon enough.

After what seemed like a long slog, they came to a fork in the tunnel. Two signs pointed either way.

The left one read: 'MAD SCIENTIST'S DESPICABLE LABORATORY'.

And the right said: 'SPINE-CHILLING FREEZER CAVE'.

'Hmmm, which way to go?' pondered Weasel, rubbing his chin. Doorkins thought right – it sounded a tiny bit less frightening. But not by much.

'Well, my friend!' exclaimed Weasel. 'What a fine opportunity for a game.'

The small mouse sighed deeply and his

shoulders slumped. Weasel did love a game –
and always chose the worst possible time for one!

'How about rock-paper-scissors? I win and
we go left. You win and we go right.'

Doorkins won three games straight. And
when Weasel insisted they went to 'winner
takes all', Doorkins won that one too.

'OK, right it is then,' sighed a resigned
Weasel, feeling a little wounded he hadn't won
at least one round.

They crept on, the temperature dropping
like a conker at autumn time. But then what
would you expect from a 'Spine Chilling
Freezer Cave'?

THUMP! Weasel was suddenly on the floor.
He had walked straight into a dead-end.

An enormous boulder covered a large hole
in the rock wall.

'Err, s-someone very big and v-very strong rolled this here,' trembled Doorkins, as he tapped the giant solid rock with his tiny claw.

'Look, Doorkins, a gap!' said Weasel excitedly, ignoring his friend's obvious concern. But was it big enough for a weasel and dormouse to squeeze through? Doorkins feared they were about to find out!

'NAAAAR!' strained Doorkins as he shoved Weasel's furry bottom through the tight opening. It took some doing, let me tell you! But Doorkins slipped inside without any problem. Dormice, you'll find, are very good at small gaps.

'It's F-F-FREEZING in here!' chattered Doorkins.

It *was* extremely chilly, thought Weasel – and also puzzlingly bare. He shone the lantern

into the dark. There was just rock, lots of ice
and the odd frosty spiderweb.

PLOP, PLOP, PLOP!

'EEEEW!' whined Doorkins as something
wet and cold dripped down his neck from above.

Weasel guided the lamp up to the ceiling.
'YIKES! FROZEN FERRET TAILS!' he
shrieked.

A big ugly mug gawped down at them, its eyes wide and a long icicle dangling from the end of its nose. It was Vic, Viv's twin brother.

Weasel moved the lantern around the rest of the cave, revealing many more familiar faces – Claus Vonberg, Half-loop McPaw, Flufftail Speedoffski. They all hung upside down from the high ceiling, frozen in by their rear paws.

Nestled in between the dozen or so animals was H, still out like a light. In shock, Weasel leaned back against the enormous slab of rock covering the cave entrance.

'What have we got ourselves into, old chum?' he sighed, wiping his weary brow.

CREAK–CRACK. UH–OH! The mighty chunk of stone blocking the entrance suddenly shifted. Weasel had the distinct feeling this would not end well. It began to tip …

CREEEEEEEEAK, SMAAAAAAASH! The rock shattered on the floor with a horrendous racket. The echo bounced down the tunnel … eventually fading into silence.

'Oops!' said Weasel with a guilty look on his chops.

'Listen,' whispered Doorkins. He aimed one of his super-dormouse ears down the gaping black tunnel.

A faint chittering noise could be heard, gradually growing louder and louder.

'Doorkins, do you still have the WI6 Mega Mittens?' asked Weasel urgently.

'Y-Yes, I think so,' said the quivering dormouse and he looked fearfully towards the approaching … well, whatever it was.

He fished around in his small leather bag and pulled out the whopping gloves. How he'd got them in there, Weasel would never know!

'Can you defrost this lot?' He gestured to the dangling captives.

'Er … how will I get up there?' The little mouse raised his eyes uncertainly to the high ceiling.

'My friend, you're a dormouse. An expert climber and all that!'

Doorkins had quite forgotten his climbing skills in all the hullabaloo. He gave a determined nod to Agent Weasel.

'Good show, old chum. I'll deal with this lot!' Weasel growled. A horde of bright red eyes appeared round the tunnel bend. He took a deep breath. 'Well, here goes nothing – again!' And he sprinted straight at the chittering wall of noise.

Weasel's eyes were getting used to the dark now. He could make out a mass of furry little bundles charging straight in his direction.

What an earth were they? Hamsters, gerbils, voles? As they bobbed up in the dim light, he noticed unusual dark splodges on their backs. CRIKEY, THEY ARE LEMMINGS! A *pack of crazed chattering lemmings.*

Weasel's options were not great. It was either a head-on collision – which didn't sound that appealing – or scoot up the tunnel's side, just beyond their gnashing teeth, leading them away from Doorkins and the freezer cave. Definitely option two!

The lemmings squeaked and spat angrily as he flashed by, just out of reach. The fierce little furballs turned on the spot, piling after him in the opposite direction.

Weasel skittered round the corner at the fork in the tunnel and glanced up at the overhead sign: 'MAD SCIENTIST'S DESPICABLE LABORATORY'. Well, spies and mad scientists always meet at some point. And this was as good a time as any, he concluded. Sticking his head down, Weasel galloped headlong into the forbidding darkness.

He glanced over his shoulder and saw the lemmings still in hot pursuit. Shaking off these dogged little rodents was not going to be easy. Increasing his pace, the super-spy began to pull away. And though Weasel didn't like to brag, he could bound along like this all day long. But if he met another dead-end, what were his chances then? Not good – not good at all!

He strained his eyes into the dark ... something did not look quite right. There appeared to be a gap in the tunnel.

YIKES! Yes, there was a gap. But more like a deep crevasse! Weasel screeched to a halt and ferreted around in his WI6 spy jumper.

After a few moments, he pulled out a ... whip. Weasel stared in ASTONISHMENT – it was exactly what he wanted. Well, that had never happened before – but there was a first time for everything!

With a skilful flick of the paw, he wrapped the whip around the nearest stalactite and gave a firm tug. Would it take his weight? He was about to find out.

Aware his pursuers were nearly on him, he swung swiftly across the wide opening … and landed on the other side. There was a real commotion behind him.

'GIDDY-GREEN-GOOSEGOGS!' he exclaimed. A number of way-too-eager lemmings must have tried to grab him as he swung and had plunged into the crevasse. He'd heard of lemmings chucking themselves over cliffs before, but he'd never actually seen it!

Weasel cocked an ear into the deep pit. There was plenty of squeaking and they sounded angry and loud enough to be OK. The others stared back from the opposite side with the same zombified expression he'd seen with the squirrels and Gerit Grouse. It was like their minds were not their own.

'Well, I'd like to hang around, my little furry friends, but I must be off.' Weasel gave a quick salute, turned and ran straight into a colossal, fluffy white wall. As he looked up, two bright-yellow saucer-shaped eyes glared down at him. It was the massive snowy owl. It opened its wings and – *SWOOOSH!* – all went black.

CHAPTER 14

Weasel awoke in a bit of a daze.

SNIFF, SNIFF! The incredibly strong smell of hot chocolate must have brought him to his senses. As his vision focused, he saw he was in some kind of laboratory. A mad scientist's despicable laboratory – if that sign was anything to go by!

At least it was a bit warmer in here. His toes were coming back to life and his nose no longer felt like an ice-pop.

He was in a large dome-shaped cavern, brightly lit, with pipes running everywhere.

High up, fixed to the rock wall, ran a platform balcony, where valves steamed and gauges pinged. Lots of little furry lemmings stood about gazing blankly. Occasionally they suddenly burst into action, tweaking dials or pulling levers, then stood stock-still again with that vacant stare.

Weasel tried to move his arms but couldn't. His itchy nose needed a darn good scratch, but that would be impossible.

He saw he was strapped into a shallow metal cage, suspended above an enormous steaming vat of hot chocolate. Marshmallows and choccie bits churned around as lemmings stirred the vat with oversized wooden spoons.

How in DANGLY DRAWERS' NAME could he get out of this one? *Stay calm, Agent Weasel*, he thought to himself.

And then it came to him – Muriel. She always got him out of a fix …

Uh-oh, he'd almost forgotten! She'd been banished to her box, over the er … wool problem. And there was no way he was wriggling that out of his WI6 spy jumper – not in his current position anyway. What if the box dropped into the swirling hot chocolate? He would never forgive himself. No, he would have to come up with another plan.

'There is no escape, Mr Weasel,' said a familiar, high-pitched croaky voice, appearing to have read the super-spy's mind.

The great white owl perched in the far corner of the cavern, fast asleep. Stood on the high balcony, gently stroking the giant bird's head, was who else but shady-mack.

'How do you like my nifty little set-up …

AGENT WEASEL?' asked the cloaked figure, waving a paw around the laboratory.

'For a mad scientist's lab, it's not too shabby,' replied Weasel matter of factly. 'Assuming you are a mad scientist. Or to be more precise ... THE ABOMINABLE DR SNOW!'

The figure's shoulders dropped. It briskly whipped off the wide-brimmed hat.

To Weasel's surprise, two long floppy ears popped up.

'Sooooo, you know my true identity?' said the floppy-eared wrongdoer cautiously.

Weasel shrugged. 'Er … no, it was just a hunch. But thanks very much for confirming it!'

'ARRRRGH!' snapped the doctor as he spun round to face the WI6 spy. He was covered in white fur from head to foot and had a jagged scar running down one side of his face below a black eyepatch. His one cruel ice-blue eye fixed Weasel with a vengeful glare.

HOPPING HICKORY NUTS, a mountain hare! Weasel might have guessed. The long hairy feet, the white fluffy tail – the clues had all been there.

'Everything was going to plan before you and your WI6 cronies turned up,' the hare spat angrily. 'Why couldn't you have just stayed away – did you not get my letters?'

'Ah yes, the letters. The glitter was a nice touch.' Weasel gave the hare a cheeky wink.

'Did you really think so? It was all my own design, you know. Nanna said leave it off, that I'd look like a fool ...' Dr Snow paused. 'Ah, you're messing with me, aren't you? Well, no matter, Agent Weasel, as you will soon be under MY CONTROL!'

'Oh really? How's that then?' Weasel said casually.

'Once lowered into this vat of mind-control hot chocolate, you will be completely within my power. Remember the grouse and the squirrels? With my cunning disguise, I brilliantly switched ordinary hot chocolate for my secret recipe. And then with one quick—'

'Flash of your camera?' interrupted Weasel. 'That's how you activate the mind control, isn't it?'

'YES!' chuckled the doctor. 'You are not as daft as you look, Agent Weasel.'

Weasel grinned, quite pleased with himself … and then realised it wasn't actually a compliment.

'My vast reserves of liquid choccie gold will soon be piped into the kiosks and cafes across Deepdip village. I will have my elite-athlete minion army. I will have total domination over the United Woodlands. MUAHAHAHA!'

Why did all super-villains have that annoying laugh? It was so predictable!

'HORATIO. HORATIO,' came a shaky old voice from some way off.

'Er … yes, Nanna, my sweet!' replied Dr Snow.

Weasel couldn't help a little snigger. The infamous doctor's real name was HORATIO SNOW.

'You had one job to do,' the doddery old voice continued. 'GET RID of those AWFUL animals in my backyard!'

'I will soon, Nanna dearest,' Dr Snow said impatiently. 'But there is the small matter of my Woodland-wide domination – it all takes time you know.'

'Well, this is my hill. And I want those Winter Whoopers gone – do you hear me?'

'Loud and clear, Nanna. And it's Whopper, not Whooper,' he replied like a moody teenager.

'Whoopers or Whoppers, I want them to disappear. And don't forget – your bath is ready.'

'Ah, y-yes, Nanna my sweet.' He sighed

and raised his eyes to the ceiling in total embarrassment.

Humhmm! Weasel struggled to hold back his laughter.

'I shall deal with YOU after my ba— Er … other business.' And off he hopped, yelling, 'Keep an eye on that one, you lot!'

The little lemmings turned at once, glaring up at the suspended super-agent.

The warm steam from the hot chocolate was making poor Weasel drowsy. After a while, he began to nod off.

I need to keep my concentration up, he told himself. *Hmmm, what about a game! What would be good for keeping the old peepers open?* he pondered. *Ah, I have it … a staring contest!* Yes, that was it. But unfortunately, there were only the lemmings.

And they hadn't blinked for at least twenty minutes – in fact, Weasel hadn't seen them blink at all yet! *Hmmm, maybe something else then ...*

'Weeeasel,' came a whisper from above. He looked up.

Peeking out from behind a massive stalactite was Woodland Ranger Blanche.

'Boy am I relieved to see you! How on earth did you find me?' he whispered.

'I'm a Woodland Ranger,' she said proudly. 'Tracking is my thing.' Weasel was getting to like this white ermine – she was definitely a good sort. 'Hang on, Weasel.' Blanche shimmied down a chain towards the cage and dropped on top. It began to gently sway, but the lemmings didn't seem to notice. Then a sudden waft of chocolaty fumes swished up towards her. Blanche got a full whiff in the snout.

AAH – AAH – AAH! She pinched her nose to stifle the sneeze – fortunately it seemed to work.

CRIKEY! Was she allergic to hot chocolate?!

'Who'd have thought,' murmured Weasel.

'YAAAACHOOOOO!' exploded Blanche.

The lemmings instantly snapped their gaze at the white ermine and began to march down the balcony steps. The furry terrors popped up one by one, on to the vat rim, clambering on their nearest crony's shoulders. They were forming a lemming tower!

'YICKERTY YIKES!' yelled Weasel. 'They'll reach us in no time!'

Blanche fiddled desperately with the catch on the back of the cage, causing it to rock wildly. There was a sudden *CLUNK!* Then the hum of a motor. The cage began to slowly move down.

Down towards the hot chocolate vat and the zombie lemmings!

CHAPTER 15

More and more lemmings piled into the despicable lab. The situation looked pretty hopeless for the captive spy and the Woodland Ranger. The cage lowered incredibly slowly, as they usually do in this kind of story – just to up the tension.

'Can we help at all?' came a voice from behind. Well, if it wasn't Corporal Steadfast and her beetle crew, hovering only a metre away.

'YES, YES, YES!' cried Weasel. 'GET THIS BLITHERING CAGE OPEN ... PLEASE.'

Trusty Magoo flexed his massive pincers and ... *PING!* The door flew open.

'Time to kick some lemming booty,' whooped Weasel, tearing the ropes from his wrists. Vicious little claws suddenly grabbed for their legs, but Weasel  and Blanche were too quick. Bounding from the wobbly cage, they plonked down on the lab floor – just as the lemming tower collapsed into the vat below. *SPUUURLOSH!*

Weasel, Blanche and the beetles were ready to scrap with the lemmings still on the ground, but they were completely surrounded by the ferocious minions. They began to creep in slowly ...

Weasel could feel the War Dance coming on. He was about to go off like a firework when ...

'CHAAAARGE!' Vic bulldozed through, batting snarling lemmings left, right and centre. Mole, Doorkins, Viv, H and the missing athletes rammed behind the great wide fox.

'Weasel, sorry about before!' Vic yelled, swatting away another rabid lemming. 'Just wanted to get to the games – all those cakes and puddings, you know.'

'No hard feelings, old chap – help me out of this pickle, and all is forgiven.'

'YOU'RE ON!' he cried.

Everyone piled in. Blanche swung round like a whirling top, taking out sets of advancing lemmings. Doorkins thrashed out with the WI6 Mega Mittens. Mole lashed her spade-like paws kung-fu style. The beetles zipped overhead, nipping lemming ears.

It was right royal battle – fierce little furballs flew here, there and everywhere. But most of the lemmings stood straight back up and came for more!

Viv used her big tummy to bounce the tiny

terrors to the far side of the lab. Even H got involved, rolling up in a ball – as hedgehogs do – and clonking them over like sets of skittles.

'STOOOOOP!' cried an anxious voice from the balcony above.

It was the Abominable Dr Horatio Snow – in his bathrobe and slippers, a pink fluffy towel wrapped around his head.

Everyone froze in an instant.

'NOOOO! What have you done to my precious mind-control chocolate?'

To be fair, he did have a point. The vat was crammed full of lemmings, bobbing around on their backs with wide trance-like stares.

The wicked scientist was not best pleased.

'DESTROY THEM. DESTROY THEM ALL!' he cried rather dramatically.

The lemmings obeyed and attacked more

fiercely than ever. It was no use – there were too many of the little fiends. The team were getting overrun.

Weasel saw Dr Snow about to chuck a barrel of chocolate sprinkles off the balcony … right on to Flufftail Speedoffski and Claus Vonberg as they battled the advancing minions below.

Agent Weasel gasped. He must save them. *Hmmm – how to get an athlete's attention?* Grabbing Doorkins's whistle from around his neck, Weasel blew a warning with all his might.

PEEEEEEEEEEEEEP!

Everything stopped dead.

The lemmings shook their heads, as though emerging from a dream. The blank stares had gone. If anything, they looked a bit puzzled.

The big snowy owl in the corner blinked, as if waking from a deep sleep. It said, in a dazed voice, 'Oh, is it still daytime?' Then closed its eyes and went straight back to sleep.

'ARGHHHHHH! DESTROY THEM. DESTROY THEM!' screeched their enraged leader.

But the little lemmings turned slowly and looked directly at the manic hare, narrowing their eyes to scowl at the doctor.

'It was HIM,' squeaked a particularly small lemming peeking over the rim of the hot chocolate vat. 'He's the one who BRAINWASHED us!'

'N-NO, MY MINIONS, I AM YOUR GLORIOUS LEADER!' cried Dr Snow hysterically. The lemmings began a steady and menacing march up the steps towards the raving scientist, who had absolutely nowhere to go.

'Please, I'll give you anything you want – loads of tender grass shoots. That's what you lot like, isn't it?' he pleaded. But the lemmings marched on.

'YAAAAH! Nanna, help, help!' the hare squealed as the little rodents lifted him overhead.

'HORATIO, keep it down,' croaked a shaky old voice. 'You could have warned me you

were having a party. Really – first these Winter Whoopers and now this! I'm going to bed ...'
The voice shuffled away down the tunnel.

'NANNA, PLEASE ... and it's *Whoppers* not Whoopers!' Dr Snow cried.

The little creatures trooped to the end of the balcony – positioning the hare right above the gurgling vat of hot chocolate.

'NOOOOOOO, not that, anything but that!'

Doorkins couldn't bear to watch, and covered his eyes with his paws.

As if throwing out a load of stinky rubbish, the lemmings tipped the white mountain hare in ... *SPLOOOOOSH!*

The abominable doctor disappeared under the hot chocolate, then finally surfaced, coughing and spluttering. Viv and Vic dragged him over the vat's rim, where one of the lemmings had set up the rickety old box-camera.

'Smile for the birdie,' the lemming said, then ... *FLASH!*

CHAPTER 16

Their mission now complete, the animals sat outside the famous Hot Choccie Emporium in Deepdip, basking in the warm winter sunshine. All had to agree – this year's Winter Whopper had been a particularly fun-filled adventure, even if it had got a bit fur-raising at times.

It had been touch and go in the lab, but the team had come out on top. All the lemmings had gone free. And the team had allowed Nanna Snow to stay in the underground lair, on one condition – strictly no brewing of dodgy concoctions.

'Well done, chaps,' Agent Weasel congratulated his team. 'I'd be a mind-controlled zombie by now, if it wasn't for you lot.' Muriel perched on his shoulder – she had forgiven Weasel for locking her up, but she wasn't really over her wool issues just yet. She sat hungrily eyeing up Doorkins's pom-pom.

It was almost time to go. The team were thinking of home and the long journey back to the United Woodlands.

'Well, I must be off now,' said Blanche, jumping up from her chair and slinging on a rucksack. 'Lots of rangering to be done back up north.'

'Are you walking all the way?' asked a concerned Doorkins.

'Noooo, of course not – I have my own sidekick now.'

A large shadow passed overhead. Then …
THWUMP! A huge white owl landed in a big
cloud of snow. The animals all jumped back
in shock!

'Is we ready to go now, Blanche?' the bird
said in a friendly, rather dopey voice.

Blanche gracefully leapt on to the owl's
fluffy back.

'Yes, time to go, Hedge-gig. See you soon, my friends!'

The bird flapped its massive wings, and Steadfast and her beetles snapped a quick salute to the brave white ermine. As the owl lifted off, Blanche blew a kiss to the surprised Weasel.

Mole gave him a little nudge and a pat on the back as the super-agent went all shy and red-faced. Weasel watched Blanche fly into the wide blue yonder … but a firm voice brought him back to his senses.

'Agent Weasel.' It was H, perched at the back of her pedal sled, flanked by her badger bodyguards. 'Wanted to say, excellent work, team,' she said rather tiredly. 'I shall expect a full report back at Hedgequarters, Agent Weasel.' She nodded to him stiffly and he gave her a strained smile. 'I'm off home now for some much needed hibernation.'

The sled was about to pull off when H turned to them again.

'Whatever happened to the Abominable Dr Snow?'

Weasel and Mole looked at each other knowingly.

'Ah, don't worry about that, ma'am – we have him … er … kept busy,' replied Mole with a little smirk.

As the sled trundled away, a look of concern spread across the head-honcho's brow.

'Right then, who's for hot chocolate?' asked Weasel, rubbing his paws together.

'Er … funnily enough, I've gone right off it,' said Doorkins. The others had to agree – even Weasel.

'Tea and biscuits all round then. WAITER!' called Weasel.

Weasel turned to find a tall white hare with a black eyepatch standing directly behind him. The creature wore a bright green Whopper Maker bib and stared unblinkingly – in a trance-like way.

'Ah, the good doctor – teas for everybody please,' said Weasel, beaming.

The hare nodded with an expressionless face. His own mind-control HC certainly seemed to have worked on him.

Viv and Vic pulled up in the WI6 pedal sled.

'Ready for the off, everyone?' asked Viv.

The animals looked to each other. They were all desperate to get back home.

'Aww, let's go,' said Weasel. The team all leapt on the sled and Weasel turned to the hare. 'Hold that order, my man – and good luck in the new job.'

Dr Snow just stared blankly at the WI6 agent.

Weasel plonked down next to Doorkins and patted his good buddy on the back. 'How goes it, old chum?'

'Fine, Weasel, fine. But I think I'm done with this coaching lark.' He laid a paw across his precious whistle. 'But just one last blow – for old time's sake!'

Before Weasel could stop him …

PEEEEEEEEEEEEEP!

Weasel looked over his shoulder as the sled pulled out of the village. A bright green Whopper Maker bib was swirling in the wind and the hare was nowhere to be seen.

GULP!

NICK EAST is the illustrator of the bestselling *Toto the Ninja Cat* as well as the *Goodnight Digger* and *Knock Knock* series. He worked for many years as a museum designer but has always been a storyteller, whether as a child, filling sketchbooks with quirky characters, or as a designer displaying a collection of ancient artefacts. He lives near York with his wife and two children and, when not writing or drawing, he is out roaming the countryside with a rucksack on his back.

NICK SAYS:

Love to my wonderful family, who put up with me
shut in the attic scribbling away for weeks on end.
A salute to the amazing Rachel and Alison
for keeping me in line with a prod or two every now
and again – you are both total stars.
Thank you so much to Dermot for your generous spirit
and encouragement – a truly wonderful gent.
To Heather: a rock of an agent and an incredible lady.
And most of all to you guys for reading the stories – the
little mustelid spy is eternally grateful and so am I.

And not forgetting the beautiful British countryside, which
just continues to astound me.